# LORDS OF THE STRATOSPHERE

# LECTOR HOUSE PUBLIC DOMAIN WORKS

This book is a result of an effort made by Lector House towards making a contribution to the preservation and repair of original classic literature. The original text is in the public domain in the United States of America, and possibly other countries depending upon their specific copyright laws.

In an attempt to preserve, improve and recreate the original content, certain conventional norms with regard to typographical mistakes, hyphenations, punctuations and/or other related subject matters, have been corrected upon our consideration. However, few such imperfections might not have been rectified as they were inherited and preserved from the original content to maintain the authenticity and construct, relevant to the work. We believe that this work holds historical, cultural and/or intellectual importance in the literary works community, therefore despite the oddities, we accounted the work for print as a part of our continuing effort towards preservation of literary work and our contribution towards the development of the society as a whole, driven by our beliefs.

We are grateful to our readers for putting their faith in us and accepting our imperfections with regard to preservation of the historical content. We shall strive hard to meet up to the expectations to improve further to provide an enriching reading experience.

Though, we conduct extensive research in ascertaining the status of copyright before redeveloping a version of the content, in rare cases, a classic work might be incorrectly marked as not-in-copyright. In such cases, if you are the copyright holder, then kindly contact us or write to us, and we shall get back to you with an immediate course of action.

**HAPPY READING!**

# LORDS OF THE STRATOSPHERE

## ARTHUR J. BURKS

ISBN: 978-93-5336-617-9

First Published:  -

© LECTOR HOUSE LLP

LECTOR HOUSE LLP
E-MAIL: lectorpublishing@gmail.com

# LORDS OF THE STRATOSPHERE
## A COMPLETE NOVELETTE

BY

## ARTHUR J. BURKS

# CONTENTS


| Chapter | Page |
|---|---|
| I. THE TAKE-OFF | 1 |
| II. THE GHOSTLY COLUMNS | 7 |
| III. STRANGE LEVITATION | 11 |
| IV. FRANTIC SCHEMING | 16 |
| V. INTO THE VOID | 21 |
| VI. STRATOSPHERE CURRENTS | 25 |
| VII. INVISIBLE GLOBE | 29 |
| VIII. CATACLYSMIC HUNGER | 35 |
| IX. A SCHEME IS DESCRIBED | 40 |
| X. HOW IT CAME ABOUT | 46 |
| XI. TO THE RESCUE | 51 |
| XII. HIGH CHAOS | 56 |

# CHAPTER I

## THE TAKE-OFF

High into air are the great New York buildings lifted by a ray whose source no telescope can find.

It seemed only fitting and proper that the greatest of all leaps into space should start from Roosevelt Field, where so many great flights had begun and ended. Fliers whose names had rung—for a space—around the world, had landed here and been received by New York with all the pomp of visiting kings. Fliers had departed here for the lands of kings, to be received by them when their journeys were ended.

Of course Lucian Jeter and Tema Eyer were disappointed that Franz Kress had beaten them out in the race to be first into the stratosphere above fifty-five thousand feet. There was a chance that Kress would fail, when it would be the turn of Jeter and Eyer. They didn't wish for his failure, of course. They were sports-men as well as scientists; but they were just human enough to anticipate the plaudits of the world which would be showered without stint upon the fliers who succeeded.

**THE WARSHIP SIMPLY VANISHED INTO THE NIGHT SKY.**

"At least, Tema," said Jeter quietly, "we can look his ship over and see if there is anything about it that will suggest something to us. Of course, whether he succeeds or fails, we shall make the attempt as soon as we are ready."

"Indeed, yes," replied Eyer. "For no man will ever fly so high that another may not fly even higher. Once planes are constructed of unlimited flying radius ... well, the universe is large and there should be no end of space fights for a long time."

Eyer, the elder of the two partner scientists, was given sometimes to quiet biting sarcasm that almost took the hide off. Jeter never minded greatly, for he knew Eyer thoroughly and liked him immensely. Besides they were complements to each other. The brain of each received from the other exactly that which he needed to supplement his own knowledge of science.

They had one other thing in common. They had been "child prodigies," but contrary to the usual rule, they had both fulfilled their early promise. Their early precocious wisdom had not vanished with the passing of childhood. Each possessed a name with which to conjure in the world of science. And each possessed that name by right of having made it famous. And yet—they were under forty.

Jeter was a slender athletic chap with deep blue eyes and brown hair. His forehead was high and unnaturally white. There was always a still sort of tenseness about him when his mind was working with some idea that set him apart from the rest of the world. You felt then that you couldn't have broken his preoccupation in any manner at all—but that if by some miracle you did, he would wither you with his wrath.

Tema Eyer was the good nature of the partnership, with a brain no less agile and profound. He was a swart fellow, straight as an arrow, black of eyes—the sort which caused both men and women to turn and look after him on the street. Children took to both men on sight.

The crowd which had come out to watch the take-off of Franz Kress was a huge one—huge and restless. There had been much publicity attendant on this flight, none of it welcome to Kress. Oh, later, if he succeeded, he would welcome publicity, but publicity in advance rather nettled him.

Jeter and Eyer went across to him as he was saying his last words into the microphone before stepping into his sealed cabin for the flight. Kress saw them coming and his face lighted up.

"Lord," he said, "I'm glad to see you two. I've something I must ask you."

"Anything you ask will be answered," said Jeter, "if Tema and I can answer it. Or granted—if it's a favor you wish."

Kress motioned people back in order to speak more or less privately with his brother scientists. His face became unusually grave.

"You've probably wondered—everybody has—why I insist on making this flight alone," he said, speaking just loudly enough to be heard above the purring of the mighty, but almost silent motor behind him. "I'll tell you, partly. I've had a feeling for the last month that ... well, that things may not turn out exactly as everybody hopes. Of course I'll blaze the way to new discoveries; yes, and I'll climb to a height of around a hundred thousand feet ... and ... and...."

Jeter and Eyer looked at each other. It wasn't like Kress to be gloomy just before doing something that no man had ever done before. He should have been smiling and happy — at least for the movietone cameras — but he wasn't even that. Certainly it must be something unusual to so concern him.

"Tell us, Kress," said Eyer.

Kress looked at them both for several moments.

"Just this," he said at last: "work on your own high altitude plane with all possible speed. If I don't come back ... take off and follow me into the stratosphere at once."

Had Kress, possessor of one of the keenest scientific minds in the world, taken leave of his senses? "If I don't come back," he had said. What did he expect to do? Fly off the earth utterly? That was silly.

But when the partners looked again at Kress they both had the same feeling. It probably wasn't as silly as it sounded. Did Kress know something he wasn't telling them? Did he really think he might ... well, might fly off the earth entirely, away beyond her atmosphere, and never return? How utterly absurd! And yet....

"Of course we'll do it," said Jeter. "We'd do it anyway, without word from you. We haven't stopped our own work because of your swiftly approaching conquest of the greater heights. But why shouldn't you come back?"

For a moment there was a look of positive dread upon Kress' face.

Then he spoke again very quietly:

"You know all the stuff that's been written about my flight," he said. "Most of it has been nonsense. How could laymen newspaper reporters have any conception of what I may encounter aloft? They've tried to make something of the recent passage of the Earth through an area of so-called shooting stars. They've speculated until they're black in the face as to the true nature of the recent bombardment of meteorites. They've pictured me as a hero in advance, doomed to death by direct attack from what they are pleased to call — after having invented them — denizens of the stratosphere."

"Yes?" said Jeter, when Kress paused.

Kress took a deep breath.

"They've come nearer than they hoped for in some guesses," he said. "Of course I don't know it, but I've had a feeling for some time. You know what sometimes happens when a man gets a sudden revolutionary idea? He concentrates on it like all get-out. Then somebody else bursts into the newspapers with the same identical idea, which in turn brings out hordes of claims to the same idea by countless other people. It's no new thing to writers and such-like gentry. They know that when they get such an idea they must act on it at once or somebody else will, because their thoughts on the subject have gone forth and impinged upon the mental receiving sets of others. Well, that's a rough idea, anyway. This idea of denizens of the stratosphere has attacked the popular imagination. You'll remember it broke in the papers *simultaneously*, in thirty countries of the world!"

A cold chill ran down the spine of Tema Eyer. He saw, in a flash, whither Kress' thoughts were tending—and when he saw that, it thrilled him, too, for it seemed to be proof of the very thing Kress was saying.

"You mean," he said hoarsely, "that you too think there may be something up there, something ... well, sensate? Some great composite thought which inspires the general dread of stratosphere denizens?"

Kress shrugged. He wouldn't commit himself, being too careful a scientist, but he hadn't hesitated to plant the idea. Jeter and Eyer both understood the thoughts which were teeming in Kress' brain.

"We'll do our part Kress," said Eyer. Lucian Jeter nodded agreement. Kress gripped their hands tightly—almost desperately, Jeter thought. Jeter was usually the leader where Eyer and himself were concerned and he thought already that he foresaw cataclysmic events.

**K**ress climbed into his plane. The vast crowd murmured. They knew he was adjusting everything inside for the days-long endurance test ahead of him. Kress had forgotten nothing. There was even a specially made cylinder, comparable to the globe which Picard had used in his historic balloon ascensions in Europe. This was attached to a parachute which, if the emergency arose, could be dropped. Kress, in the ball, could pass through the sub-arctic cold of the stratosphere if necessity demanded. The ball, if it struck the ocean, would preserve him for a great length of time. It was even equipped with rockets.

This plane was revolutionary. It was, to begin with, carrying a vast load. Kress was taking every conceivable kind of instrument he fancied he might need. There was food as for a long siege.

Jeter shuddered. Why had he thought of the word "siege"?

The great load would be carried without difficulty, however, for this plane was little short of a miracle. Among other things, Kress would be able, in case of fatigue, to set his controls—as at sea a pilot may sometimes lash his wheel—and sleep while his plane mounted on up, and up, in great spirals.

Up beyond fifty-five thousand he hoped to attain a thousand miles an hour velocity. That meant, say, breakfast in New York, lunch in London, tea in Novo-Sibirsk, dinner in Yokohama—as soon as the myriad planes which would follow this one in design and capabilities took off on the trail Kress was blazing.

Jeter sighed at the thought. For several years he had explored little-known sections of the world. He had visited every country. He had entered every port that could be reached from the ocean—and all the time he had felt the Earth shrinking before the gods of speed. The time would soon come when everything on

Earth would be commonplace. Then man's urge to go places he hadn't seen before would take him away from the Earth entirely—when he would begin the task of making even the universe shrink to appease the gods of speed. Somehow the thought was a melancholy one.

Now the crowd gave back as Kress speeded up his motor, indicating that he would soon take off. Jeter and Eyer studied the outward outline of Kress' craft. It looked exactly like a black beetle which has just alighted after flight, but has not yet quite hidden its wings. It was black, probably because it was believed a black object could be followed easier from the Earth.

There would be many anxious eyes watching that spiraling ship as it grew smaller and smaller, climbing upward.

With a rush, and a spinning of dust in the slipstream, the ship was away. It lifted as easily as a bird and mounted with great speed. It was capable of climbing in wide spirals at a hundred and fifty miles an hour.

A great sigh burst from the thousands who had come to watch history made. For solid hours now they would watch the plane climb, growing smaller, becoming a speck, vanishing. Many curious ones would stay right here until Kress returned, fearful of being cheated of a great thrill. For Kress was to land right here when, and if, he had conquered the stratosphere.

J eter and Eyer wormed their way through the crowd to the road and found their car in a jam of other cars. Without a word they climbed in and drove themselves to their dwelling—combined home and laboratory—in Mineola. There they fell to on their own ship, which was being built piece by piece in their laboratory.

Every half hour or so one or the other would go to the lawn and gaze aloft, seeking Kress.

"He's out of eyesight," said Eyer, the last to go. "Is the telescope set up?"

"Yes, and arranged to cover all the area of sky through which Kress is likely to climb."

At intervals through the night, long after they had ceased work, the partners rose from bed and sought their fellow scientist among the stars. They alternated at this task.

"According to my calculations," said Jeter, when the eastern sky was just paling into dawn, "Kress has now reached a point higher than man has ever flown before, higher than any living—"

Jeter stopped on the word. Both men remembered Kress' last words. Kress, upset or not, properly or improperly, had hinted of living things in the stratosphere—perhaps utterly malignant entities.

It was just here, in the dawning of the first day after Kress' departure, that the dread began to grow on Jeter and Eyer. And during the day they labored like Trojans at their work, as though to forget it.

The world had begun its grim wait for the return of Kress.

They waited all that day ... and the next ... and the next!

Then telegraph and radio, at the suggestion of Jeter, instructed the entire civilized world to turn its eyes skyward to watch for the return of Kress.

The world obeyed *that* day ... and the next ... *and the next*!

But Kress did not return; nor, so far as the world knew, did any or all of his great airplane.

The world itself began to have a feeling of dread—that grew.

# CHAPTER II

## THE GHOSTLY COLUMNS

Franz Kress had been gone a week, when all the world knew that he couldn't possibly have stayed aloft that length of time. Yet no word was received from him, no report received from any part of the world that he had returned. Various islands which he might have reached were scoured for traces of him. The lighter vessels of most of the navies of the world joined in the search to no avail. Kress had merely mounted into the sky and vanished.

The world's last word from him had been a few words on the radio-telephone:

"Have reached sixty thousand feet and—"

There the message had ended, as though the speaker, eleven miles above the earth, had been strangled. Yet he didn't drop, as far as anybody in the world knew.

Lucian Jeter and Tema Eyer worked harder than ever, remembering the promise they had made Kress at his take-off. Whatever had happened to him, he seemingly in part had anticipated. And now the partners would go up, too, seeking information—perhaps to vanish as Kress had vanished. They were not afraid. They shared the world's feeling of dread, but they were not afraid. Of course death would end their labors, but there were many scientists in the world to take up where they might leave off.

There were, for example, Sitsumi of Japan, rumored discoverer of a substance capable of bending light rays about itself to render itself invisible; Wang Li, Liao Wu, Yung Chan, of China—three who had degrees from the world's greatest universities and had added miraculously to the store of knowledge by their own inspired research. These three were patriotically eager to bring China back to her rightful place as the leader in scientific research—a place she had not held for a thousand years. It was generally agreed among scientists that the three would shortly outstrip all their contemporaries.

As Jeter thought of these four men, Orientals all, it suddenly occurred to him to communicate with them. He talked it over with Eyer and decided to send carefully worded cables to all four.

In a few hours he received answers to them:

From Japan: "Sitsumi does not care to communicate." There was a world of cold hostility in the words, Jeter thought, and Eyer agreed with him.

From China came the strangest message of all:

"Wang, Liao and Yung have been cut off from world for past four months, conducting confidential research in Gobi laboratories. Impossible to communicate because area in which laboratories situated in Japanese hands and surrounded by cordon of guards."

Jeter and Eyer stared at each other when the cable had been read and digested.

"Queer, isn't it?" said Eyer.

Jeter didn't answer. That preoccupied expression was on his face, that distant look which no man could erase from his face by any interruption until Jeter had finished his train of thought.

"Queer," thought Jeter, "that Sitsumi should be so snooty and the three Chinese totally unavailable."

There were many strange things happening lately, too, and the queer things kept on happening, and in ever-increasing numbers, during the second week of Kress' impossible absence in the stratosphere. Or was he there? Had he ever reached it? Had he—Jeter and Eyer had noticed his utter gloom at the take-off—merely, climbed out of sight of the Earth and then slanted down to a dive into the ocean? Maybe he was a suicide. But some bits of wreckage of his plane had many unsinkable parts about it—the parachute ball for instance.

No, the solemn fact remained that Kress had simply flown up and hadn't come down again. It would have sounded silly and absurd if it hadn't been so serious.

And strange stories were seeping into the press of the world.

Out in Wyoming a cattleman had driven a herd of prime steers into the round-up corral at night. Next morning not one of the steers could be found. No tracks led away from the corral. The gates were closed, exactly as they had been left the night before. There had been no cowboys watching the steers, for the corral had always been strong enough to hold the most rambunctious.

The tale of the missing steers hit the headlines, but so far nobody had thought of this disappearance in connection with Kress'. How could any one? Steers and scientists didn't go together. But it still was strange.

At least so Jeter thought. His mind worked with this and other strange happenings even as he and Eyer worked at top speed.

A young fellow in Arizona told a yarn of wandering about the crater of a meteor which had fallen on the desert thousands of years before. The place wasn't important nor did it seem to have anything to do with the crater or meteors—but the young fellow reported that he had seen a faded white column of light, like the beam of a great searchlight, reaching up into the sky from somewhere on the desert.

When people became amazed at his story he added to it. There had been five columns of light instead of one. The one he had first mentioned had touched the Earth, or had shot up from the Earth, within several miles of his point of vantage.

A second glowed off to the northwest, a third to the southwest, a fourth to the southeast, the fifth to the northeast. The first one seemed to "center" the other four—they might have been the five legs of a table, according to their arrangement....

Arrangement! Jeter wondered how that word had happened to come to him.

The story of the fellow who had seen the columns of light might have been believed if he had stuck to his first yarn of seeing but one. But when he mentioned five ... well, he didn't have any too good a reputation for veracity and wasn't regarded as being overly bright. Besides, he had stated that the thickness of the columns of light seemed to be the same from the ground as far as his eyes could follow them upward. Everybody knew that a searchlight's beams spread out a bit.

"I wonder," thought Jeter, "why the kid didn't say he saw those five columns move—like a five-legged animal, walking."

Silly, of course, but behind the silliness of the thought Jeter thought there might be something of interest, something on which to work.

The Jeter-Eyer space ship still was not finished—though almost—when the world moved into the third week since the disappearance of Franz Kress.

An Indian in the Southwest had reported seeing one of those columns of light. However, this merited just a line on about page sixteen, even of the newspaper closest to the spot where the redskin had seen the column.

"Eyer," said Jeter at last, "we've got to start digging into newspaper stories, especially into stories which deal with unusually queer happenings throughout the world. I've a hunch that the keys to Kress' disappearance may be found in some of them, or a combination of a great many of them."

"How do you mean, Lucian?"

"Don't you notice that all this queer stuff has been happening since Kress left? It sounds silly, perhaps, but I feel sure that the disappearance of those steers in Wyoming, the story the boy told about the columns of light—yes, all five of them!—and the Indian's partial confirmation of it, are all tied up together with the disappearance of Kress."

Eyer started to grin his disbelief, but a look at his partner's tense face stopped him.

"What could want all those steers, Lucian?" said Eyer softly. "I can't think of anything or anybody disposing of such a bunch on such short notice, except a marching army, a marching column of soldier ants, or all the world's buzzards gathered together at one place. In any case the animals themselves would have created a fuss, would have kicked up so much noise that somebody would have heard. But this story of the steers seems to suggest, or say right out loud—though I know you can't believe everything in the newspapers—that the steers vanished in utter silence."

"Doesn't it also seem funny to you," went on Jeter, "that the vanishing of the herd wasn't discovered until next morning? I've read enough Western stuff to know that a herd always makes noise. Yes, even at night. The cowhands wouldn't have lost a wink of sleep over that. But, listen, Tema, suppose you lived in New York City near some busy intersection which was always noisy, even after midnight—and all the noise suddenly stopped. Would you sleep right on through it?"

"No, I'd wake up—unless I were drunk or doped."

"Yet nobody seems to have wakened at that ranch when—and it must have happened—the herd stopped making any noise whatever. The utter silence *should* have wakened seasoned cowhands. It didn't. Why? What happened to them that they slept so soundly they heard nothing?"

Eyer did not answer. It wasn't the first time he had been called upon to hear Jeter think out loud.

"It all ties up somehow," repeated Jeter, "and I intend to find out how."

But he didn't find out. Strange stories kept appearing. The three Chinese scientists still had not communicated with the outside world. The chap out in Arizona had now so elaborated on his yarn that nobody believed him and the public lost interest—all save Jeter, who was on the trail of a queer idea.

Nothing happened however until near the end of the third week after Kress' disappearance.

Then, out of a clear sky almost, Kress came back.

He came down by parachute, without the ball in which he should have sealed himself. His return caused plenty of comment. There was good reason. He had been gone the impossibly long period of three weeks.

He was dead—but *had* been for less than seventy-two hours!

His body was frozen solid.

It landed on the roof of the Jeter-Eyer laboratory; had he been alive he couldn't possibly have maneuvered his chute to land him on such a small place.

The partners stared at each other. It seemed strange to them indeed that Kress should have come back to land on the roof of the two who had promised to follow him into the stratosphere if he didn't return.

Very strange indeed.

He had returned, though, releasing Jeter and Eyer from their promise. Strangely enough that fact made them all the more determined to go. And while the newspaper reporters went wild over Kress' return, the partners started making additional plans.

# CHAPTER III
## STRANGE LEVITATION

"In two days we'll be ready, Tema," said Lucian Jeter quietly. "And make no mistake about it; when we take off for the stratosphere we're going to encounter strange things. Nobody can tell me that Kress' plane actually flew three weeks! And where did it come down? Why didn't Kress use the parachute ball? Where is it? I'll wager we'll find answers to plenty of those questions—if we live!"

"If we live?" repeated Eyer. "You mean—?"

"You know what happened to Kress? Or rather you know the result of what happened to him?"

"Sure."

"Why should we be immune? I tell you, Eyer, we're on the eve of something colossal, awe-inspiring—perhaps catastrophic."

Eyer grinned. Jeter grinned back at him. If they knew they flew inescapably to death they still would have grinned. They had plenty of courage.

"We'd better go into town for a meeting with newspaper people," went on Jeter. "You know how things go in the news; there are probably plenty of stories which for one reason or another have not been published. Maybe the law has clamped down on some of them. I've a feeling that if everything were told, the whole world would be frightened stiff. And you notice how quickly the papers finished with the Kress' thing."

Eyer knew, all right. The papers had broken the story of the return in flaming scareheads. Then the thing had come to a full stop. It was significant that no real satisfactory explanation had been offered by any one. The papers had, on their own initiative, tried to communicate with Sitsumi, and the three Chinese scientists, and had failed all around. Sitsumi did not answer, denied himself to representatives of the American press in Japan, and crawled into an impenetrable Oriental shell. The three Chinese could not answer, according to advices from Peking, because they could not be located.

Jeter called the publisher of the leading newspaper for a conference.

"Strange that you should have called just now," said the publisher, "for I was on the point of calling you and Eyer and inviting you to a conference to be held this evening at my office in Manhattan."

"What's the purpose of your conference? Who will attend?"

"I—I—well, let us say I had hoped to make you and Eyer available to all interviewers on the eve of your flight into the stratosphere."

Jeter hesitated, realizing that the publisher did not wish to tell everything over the telephone.

"We'll be right along, sir," he said.

It took an hour for them to reach the publisher's office. Wires had plainly been pulled, too, for a motorcycle escort joined them at the Queensboro Bridge and led them, sirens screaming, to their meeting with George Hadley, the publisher.

They looked at each other in surprise when they were admitted to the meeting.

Hadley's huge offices were packed. The mayor was there, the police commissioner, the assistant to the head of Federal Secret Service. The State Governor had sent a representative. All the newspapers had their most famous men sitting in. Right in this one big room was represented almost the entire public opinion of the United States. American representatives of foreign newspapers were there. And there wasn't a smile on a single face.

It was beginning to be borne in upon everybody that the Western Hemisphere was in the grip of a strange unearthly malady—almost an *other*-earthly malady, but what was it?

Hadley nodded to the two scientists and they took the seats he indicated.

Hadley cleared his throat and spoke.

"We have here people who represent the press of the world," he said. "We have men who control billions in money. I don't know how many of you have thought along the same lines as I have, but I feel that after I have finished speaking most of you will. First, there are certain news stories which, for reasons of policy, never reach the pages of our papers. I shall now tell you some of them...."

The whole crowd shifted slightly in its chairs. There was a strained leaning forward. Grave faces went whiter as they anticipated gripping announcements.

"All the strange things have not been happening in the United States, gentlemen," said Hadley. "That young fellow who reported seeing the columns of light in Arizona—you remember?—"

There was a chorus of nods.

"He probably told the exact truth, as far as he knew it. But it isn't only in Arizona that it has been seen—those columns I mean. Only there is just one column—not five. It has since been reported in Nepal and Bhutan, in Egypt and Morocco and a dozen other places. But in the cases of such stories emanating from foreign countries, a congress of publishers has withheld the facts, not because of their strangeness but because of the effect they might have on the public sanity. In Nepal, for example, the column of light rested for a moment on an ancient temple, and when the light vanished the temple also had vanished, with everybody in it at the time for worship! Rumor had it that some of the worshipers were later found and identified. They appear to have been scattered over half of Nepal—and every last one was smashed almost to a pulp, as though the body had been dropped from an enormous height."

A concerted gasp raced around the assemblage. Then silence again, while the pale-faced Hadley went on with his unbelievable story.

"**A**mad story comes from the heart of the *terai*, in India. I don't know what importance to give this story since the only witnesses to the phenomenon were ignorant natives. But the column of light played into the *terai*—and tigers, huge snakes, buffalo and even elephants rose bodily over the treetops and vanished. They started up slowly—then disappeared with the speed of light."

"Were crushed animals later found in the jungle?" asked Jeter quietly.

Hadley turned his somber eyes on the questioner. Every white face, every fearful eye, also turned toward Jeter.

And Hadley nodded.

"It's too much to be coincidence," he said. "The crushed and broken bodies in Nepal and India—of course they aren't so far apart but that natives in either place might have heard the story from the other—but I am inclined to believe in the inner truth of the stories in each case."

Hadley turned to the two scientists. There were other scientists present, but the fact that Jeter and Eyer, who were so soon to follow Kress into the stratosphere—and eternity?—held the places of honor near the desk of the spokesman, was significant.

"What do you gentlemen think?" asked Hadley quietly.

"There is undoubtedly some connection between the two happenings," said Jeter. "I think Eyer and myself will be able to make some report on the matter soon. We will, take off for the stratosphere day after to-morrow."

"Then you think the same thing I do?" said Hadley. "If that is so, can't you start to-morrow? God knows what may happen if we delay longer—though what two of you can do against something which appears to blanket the earth, and strikes from the heavens, I don't know. And yet, the fate of your country may be in your hands."

"We realize that," said Jeter, while Eyer nodded.

Hadley opened his mouth to make some other observation, then closed it again, tightly, as a horrible thing happened.

The conference was being held on the tenth floor of the Hadley building. And just as Hadley started to speak the whole building began to shake, to tremble as with the ague. Jeter turned his eyes on the others, to see their faces blurred by the vibration of the entire building.

Swiftly then he looked toward the windows of the big room.

Outside the south windows he witnessed an unbelievable thing. Out there was a twelve-story building, and its lighted windows were moving—not to right or left, but straight up! The movement gave the same impression which passing windows give to one in an elevator. Either that other building was rising straight into the air, or the Hadley building was sinking into the Earth.

"Quick, Hadley!" yelled Jeter. "To the roof the fastest way possible!"

Even as Jeter spoke every last light in the building across the way went out. Jeter knew then that it was the other building that was moving—and that electrical connection with the earth had been severed.

Hadley led the way to the roof, four stories above. Fortunately this was an old building and they didn't have to wait to travel a hundred floors or so. The whole conference followed at the heels of Hadley, Jeter and Eyer.

They reached the roof at top speed.

They were first conscious of the cries of despair, of disbelief, of horror which rose from the street canyons below them. But they forgot these the next instant at what they saw.

The Vandercook building, the twelve-story building whose lights Jeter had seen moving, was rising bodily, straight out of the well which had been built around it. From the building came shrieks and cries of mortal terror. Even as the conference froze to horrified immobility, many men and women stepped to the ledges of those darkened windows and plunged out in their fear.

"God!" said Hadley.

"It's just as well," said Jeter in a far-away voice, "they haven't a chance anyway!"

"I know," replied Hadley. "God, Jeter, isn't there something we can do?"

"I hope to find something," said Jeter. "But just now I'm afraid we are helpless."

The Vandercook building continued to rise. It did not totter; it simply rose in its entirety, leaving the gaping hole into which, decades ago, it had been built. It rose straight into the sky, apparently of its own volition. No rays of light, no supernatural agencies could be seen or fancied. The utterly impossible was happening. A building was a-wing.

Jeter and Eyer looked at each other with protruding eyes.

Then they looked back at the Vandercook, whose base now was on a level with the roof of the Hadley building.

"See?" said Hadley. "Not so much as a brick falls from the foundation. It's—

it's—ghastly."

Jeter would never forget the screams of mortal terror which came from the lips of the doomed who had been working late in the Vandercook building—for, horror piled upon horror, those who had sought to escape calamity did not fall to Earth at all, but, at the same speed of the rising building, traveled skyward with it, human flies outside those leering dark windows.

Then, free of New York's skyline, the flying building was gone with a rush. A thousand feet above New York's tallest building, the Vandercook changed direction and moved directly into the west.

The conference watched it go....

"Commissioner," Jeter yelled at the police chief of Manhattan, "get word out at once for all lights to be put out in the city! Hurry! Radio would be fastest."

In ten minutes Manhattan was a darkened, silent city ... and now the conference could see why Jeter had asked for all lights to be extinguished.

Five thousand feet aloft, directly over the Hudson River, the Vandercook building now hung motionless—and all eyes saw the thin column of light. It came down from the dark skies from a vast distance, widening to encompass the top of the Vandercook building.

The Vandercook building might almost have been a mouse caught in the talons of some unbelievable night-hawk.

As though some intellect had just realized the significance of New York's sudden darkness; as though that intellect had realized that the column was ordinarily invisible because of Manhattan's brilliant incandescents, and now was visible in the darkness—the column of light snapped out....

"God Almighty! May the Lord of Hosts save the world from destruction!"

From New York's canyons, from the roof of the Hadley building, came the great composite prayer.

A whistling shriek, growing second by second into enormous proportions, came out of the west, above the Hudson.

# CHAPTER IV

## FRANTIC SCHEMING

There was no mistaking the meaning of that whistling shriek. Whatever agency had held the Vandercook building aloft had now released its uncanny grip on the building, and thousands of tons of brick and mortar, of stone and steel, were plunging down in a mass from five thousand feet above the Hudson. The same force had also released the ill-fated men and women who had been carried aloft with the building. And there must have been hundreds of people inside side the building.

It fell as one piece, that great building. It didn't topple until it had almost reached the river and its shrieking plunge became meteor-like, the sound of its fall monstrous beyond imagining. The conference above the Hadley building fancied they could feel the outward rush of air displaced by the falling monster—and drew back in fear from the edge of the roof.

The Vandercook struck the surface of the Hudson and an uprush of geysering water for a few seconds blotted the great building from view. Then all Manhattan seemed to shudder. Most of it was perhaps fancy, but thousands of frightened Manhattanites saw that fall, heard the whistling, and felt the trembling of immovable Manhattan.

The great columns of water fell back into the turbulent Hudson which had received the plunging building. Not so much as a wooden desk showed above the surface as far as any one could see from shore. Not a soul had been saved. Shrieks of the doomed had never stopped from the moment the Vandercook building had started its mad journey aloft.

Jeter whirled on Hadley.

"Will you see that all my suggestions are carried out, Hadley?" he demanded.

Hadley, face gray as ashes, nodded.

From Manhattan rose the long abysmal wailing of a populace just finding its voice of fear after a stunning, numbing catastrophe.

"I'll do whatever you say, Jeter," said Hadley. "We all agreed before the arrival of Eyer and yourself that your advice would be followed if you chose to give any."

"Then listen," said Jeter, while Eyer stood quietly at his elbow, missing nothing. "Advise the people of New York to quit the city as quietly and in as orderly a manner as possible. Let the police commissioner look after that. Then get word to the leading aviation authorities, promoters, and fliers and have them get to our Mineola laboratory as fast as possible. We've kept much of the detail of construction of our space-ship secret, for obvious reasons. But the time has come to forget personal aggrandizement and the world must know all we have learned by our labor and research. Then see that every manufacturing agency, capable of even a little of what it will take for the program, is drafted to the work—by Federal statute if necessary—and turn out copies of our plane as quickly as God will let you."

Hadley's eyes were bulging. So were those of the others who had crowded close to listen. They seemed to think Jeter had taken leave of his senses, and yet— all had seen the Vandercook building perform the utterly impossible.

Hadley nodded.

"What do you want with the filers and others at your laboratory?"

"To listen to the details of construction of our space ship. Eyer will hold a couple of classes to explain everything. Then, when we've made things as clear as possible, Eyer and I will take off and get up to do our best to counteract the—whatever it is—that seems to be ruling the stratosphere. We'll do everything possible to hold the influences in check until you can send up other space ships to our assistance."

Hadley stared.

"You speak as though you expected to be up for a long time. Planes like yours aren't made overnight."

"Planes like ours must be made almost overnight—and have you forgotten that Kress was gone for three weeks, and yet had been dead but seventy-two hours when he landed on our roof? Incidentally, Hadley, that fall of his was guided by something or someone. He didn't fall on our roof by chance. He was dropped there, as a challenge to us!"

"That means?" said Hadley hoarsely.

"That everything we do is known to the intelligence of the stratosphere! That every move we make is watched!"

"God!" said Hadley.

Then Hadley straightened. His jaws became firm, his eyes lost their fear. He was like a good soldier receiving orders.

"All the power of the press will be massed to get the country to back your suggestions, Jeter. They seem good to me. Now get back to your ship and leave everything to me. Suppose you do encounter some intelligence in the stratosphere? How will you combat it, especially if it proves inimical—which to-night's horror would seem to prove?"

Jeter shrugged.

"We'll take such armament as we have. We have several drums of a deadly volatile gas. We have guns of great power, hurling projectiles of great velocity;

but I feel all of that will be more or less useless. The intelligence up there—well, it knows everything we know and far more besides, for do any of us know how to strike at the earth from the stratosphere? Therefore our only weapons must be our own intelligence—at least that will be the program for Eyer and me. Later, when your planes which are yet to be built follow us up the sky, perhaps they will be better armed. I hope to be able to communicate information somehow, relative to whatever we find."

Hadley thrust out his hand.

"Good luck," he said simply.

T hen he was gone and Jeter and Eyer were dropping swiftly down in the elevator to the street—to find that the streets of Manhattan had gone mad. The ban on electric lights had been lifted, and the faces of fear-ridden men and women were ghastly in the brilliance of thousands of lights. Traffic accidents were happening on every corner, at every intersection, and there were all too few police to manage traffic.

However, a motorcycle squad was ready to lead the way through the press for Eyer and Jeter—two grim-faced men now, who dared not look at each other, because each feared to show his abysmal fear to the other.

Automobiles raced past on either side of them driven by crazy men and hysterical women.

"Queensboro Bridge will be packed tight as a drum," said Eyer quietly.

Jeter didn't seem to hear. Eyer talked on softly, unbothered by Jeter's silence, knowing that Jeter wouldn't hear a word, that his partner had drawn into himself and was even now, perhaps, visualizing what they might encounter in the stratosphere. Eyer talked to give shape to his own thoughts.

A world gone mad, a world that fled from the menace which hung over Manhattan.... Jeter hoped that the calm brains of men like Hadley would at least be able to quiet the populace somewhat, else many of them would be self-destroyed, as men and women destroy one another in rushes for the exits during great theater fire alarms.

Fast as they traveled, some of the foremost airmen of the adjoining country had reached Mineola ahead of them. They understood that many of them had arrived by plane in obedience to word broadcast by Hadley. Hadley was doing his bit with a vengeance.

The partners reached their laboratory.

Their head servant met them at the door.

"A Mr. Hadley frantically telephoning, sir," he said to Jeter.

Jeter listened to Hadley's words—which were not so frantic now, as though Hadley had been numbed by the awful happenings.

"The new bridge between Manhattan and Jersey," said Hadley, "has just been lifted by whatever the unearthly force is. It was pulled up from its very foundations. It was crowded with cars as people fled from New York—and cars and people were lifted with the bridge. Awful irony was in the rest of the event. The great bridge was simply turned, along its entire length—which remained intact during the miracle—until it was parallel with the river and directly above midstream. Then it was dropped into the water."

"No telling how many lives were lost?" asked Jeter.

"No, and hundreds and thousands of lives are being lost every moment now. Frantic thousands are swamping boats of all sizes in their craze to get away. Dozens of overloaded vessels have capsized and the surface of the river is alive with doomed people, fighting the water and one another...."

Jeter clicked up the receiver on the horror, knowing there was nothing he could do. There would be no end to the loss of life until some measure of sanity had been argued into crazed humanity.

All the time he kept wondering.

What was doing all this awful business? He surmised that some anti-gravitational agency was responsible for the levitation of the Vandercook building, but what sort of intelligence was directing it? Was the intelligence human? Bestial? Maniacal? Or was it something from Outside? Jeter did not think the latter could be considered. He didn't believe that any planet, possibly inhabited, was close enough to make a visit possible. At any rate, he felt that there should be some sort of warning. He held to the belief that the whole thing was caused by human, and earthly, intelligence.

But why? The world was at peace. And yet....

Thousands of lives had been snuffed out, a twelve-story building had leaped five thousand feet into the air, and the world's biggest bridge had turned upstream as though turning its back against the mad traffic it had at last been called upon to bear.

Eyer was going over their plane with the visitors, men of intellect who were taking notes at top speed, men who knew planes and were quick to grasp new appliances.

"Have any of you got the whole story now?" Eyer asked.

A half dozen men nodded.

"Then pass your knowledge on to the others. Jeter and I must get ready to be off. Every minute we delay costs untold numbers of lives."

Willing hands rolled their ship out to their own private runway, while Jeter and Eyer made last minute preparations. There was the matter of food, of oxygen necessary so far above the Earth, of clothing. All had been provided for and their last duties were largely those of checking and rechecking, to make sure no fatal errors in judgment had been made.

Eyer was to fly the ship in the beginning.

A small crowd watched as the partners, white of face now in the last minutes of their stay on Earth—which they might never touch again in life—climbed into their cabin, which was capable of being sealed against the cold of the heights and the lack of breathable oxygen.

Nobody smiled at them, for the world had stopped smiling.

Nobody waved at them, for a wave would have been frivolous.

Nobody cheered or even shouted—but the two knew that the best wishes, the very hopes for life, of all the land, went with them into the ghastly unknown.

# CHAPTER V

## INTO THE VOID

Their watches and the clock in the plane were synchronized with Hadley's time, which was Eastern Standard, and as soon as the plane had reached eight thousand feet altitude, Jeter spoke into the radiophone and arranged for a connection with the office of Hadley.

Hadley himself soon spoke into Jeter's ear.

"Yes, Jeter?"

"See that someone is always at your radiophone to listen to us. I'll keep you informed of developments as long as possible. Everything is running like clockwork so far. How is it with you?"

"Two additional buildings, older buildings of the city, have been lifted some hundreds of feet above ground level, then dropped back upon their own foundations, to be broken apart. Many lives lost despite the fact that the city will be deserted within a matter of hours. It seems that the—shall we say enemy?—is concentrating only on old buildings."

"Perhaps they wish to preserve the new ones," said Jeter quietly.

"What? Why?"

"For their own use, perhaps; who knows? Keep me informed of every eventuality. If the center of force which seems to be causing all this havoc shifts in any direction, advise us at once."

"All right, Jeter."

Jeter broke the connection temporarily. Hadley could get him at any moment. A buzzer would sound inside the almost noiseless cabin when anyone wished to contact him over the radiophone.

Eyer was concentrating on the controls. The plane was climbing in great sweeping spirals. Its speed was a hundred and fifty miles an hour. Their air speed indicator was capable of registering eight hundred miles an hour. They hoped to attain that speed and more, flying on an even keel above ninety thousand feet.

Both Eyer and Jeter were perfect navigators. If, as they hoped, they could reach ninety thousand or more, they could cross the whole United States in four hours or less. They could quarter the country, winged bloodhounds of space, seeking their quarry.

Jeter studied the sky above them through their special telescopes, seeking some hint of the location of the point of departure of that devastating column of light. He could think of no ray that would nullify gravitation—yet that column of light had been the visual manifestation that the thing had somehow been brought about.

If this were true, was the enemy vulnerable? Was his base of attack capable of being destroyed or crippled if anything happened to the column of light? There was no way of knowing—yet. A search of the sky above Manhattan failed to disclose any visible substance from which the light beam might emanate. That seemed to indicate some unbelievable height. Yet, Kress must have reached that base. Else why had he been destroyed and sent back to Jeter and Eyer as a challenge?

Jeter's mind went back to Kress. Frozen solid ... but that could have been caused by his downward plunge through space. And what had happened to Kress' plane? No word had been received concerning it up to the time of the Jeter-Eyer departure. Had the "enemy" taken possession of it?

The whole thing seemed absurd. Nobody knew better than Jeter that he was working literally and figuratively in the dark. He was doing little better than guessing. He felt sure of but one thing, that the agency which was wreaking the havoc was a human one, and he was perfectly willing to match his wits and Eyer's against any human intelligence.

Jeter slipped into the cushioned seat beside Eyer.

The altimeter registered fifteen thousand feet. New York was just a blur against the abysmal darkness under their careening wings.

"You've never ventured an opinion, Tema," said Jeter softly, "even to me."

Eyer grinned.

"Who knows?" he said. "It may all be just the very latest thing in aerial attack. If so, what country or coalition of countries harbor designs against our good Uncle Sam? Japan? China?"

"How do you explain the Vandercook incident? The bridge thing? The rise and fall of the other skyscrapers?"

"Some substance or ray capable of being controlled and directed. It creates a field, of any size desired, in which gravitation is—well, shall we say erased? Then any solid which is thus made weightless could be lifted by the two good hands of a strong man, or even of a weak one. How does that check with your guessing?"

Jeter shook his head ruefully.

"I've arrived at the same conclusions as yourself, Tema," he said. "I know we're all guessing. I know we're probably climbing off the Earth on a wild-goose chase from which we haven't a chance of returning alive. I know we're a pair of fools to think of matching a few drums of gas and a bunch of popguns against the equipment of an enemy capable of moving mountains—but what else is there to do?"

"Nothing," said Eyer cheerfully, "and I've got a feeling that you and I will manage to acquit ourselves with credit."

The radiophone buzzer sounded.

Hadley was speaking.

"One of the very latest types of battle-wagons," he said, "was steaming this way from the open sea outside the Narrows, ordered here to stand by in case of need, by the Navy Department. She was armed to the minute with the very latest ordnance. She carried a full crew...."

**H**adley paused. Jeter could hear him take a deep breath, like a diver preparing to plunge into icy water. Jeter's spine tingled. He felt he guessed in advance what was to come.

Hadley went on.

The world seemed to spin dizzily as Jeter listened. Out of all the madness only one thing loomed which served for the moment to keep Jeter sane. That was the altimeter, which registered twenty-five thousand feet.

"The battle-wagon—the *U.S.S. Hueber*—was yanked bodily out of the water. It was taken aloft so quickly that it was just a blur. At least this was the way the skipper of a Norwegian steamer, a mile away from the *Hueber*, described it. The warship simply vanished into the night sky. The exact time was given by the Norwegian. Five minutes before midnight. At that moment nothing was happening in New York City—nothing new, that is."

Hadley paused again.

"Go on, man!" said Jeter hoarsely.

"Twenty minutes later the *Hueber* was lowered back into the water, practically unharmed. It had all happened so swiftly that the sailors aboard scarcely realized anything had happened. The skipper of the warship radios that the sensation was like a sudden attack of dizziness. One man died of heart failure. He was the only casualty."

Jeter's eyes began to blaze with excitement, as he spoke.

"Now you can tell the world that the thing which causes the havoc Manhattan is experiencing is not supernatural. It is human—and our people have no fear of human enemies."

"But why was not the warship dropped somewhere, as the buildings have been?" asked Hadley.

"Did you ever," replied Jeter, "hear what is described in the best fiction as a burst of ironic laughter? Well, that what the *Hueber*, as it now stands, or floats, is! But the enemy made a foolish move and will live to regret it bitterly."

"I wish I could share your sudden confidence," said Hadley. "Conditions here, where public morale is concerned, have become more frightful minute by minute since you left."

Jeter severed the connection.

 he altimeter said thirty-five thousand feet. They were still spiraling upward. Again Jeter surveyed the sky aloft.

The earth below was a blur, save through the telescopes. The two had reached a height less than a third of what they hoped to attain.

Still they could see nothing up above them. They were almost over the "shaft" of atmosphere through which the *Hueber* must have been lifted and lowered. Suppose, Jeter thought, they had accidentally flown into that shaft at exactly the wrong moment? It brought a shudder. Still, Jeter's mind went on, if that had happened they would now, in all likelihood, have been right among the enemy—for gravity in that shaft would not have existed for them, either.

But would they have been lowered back to safety as the *Hueber* and her crew had been?

Believing as he did that the enemy knew everything that transpired within its sphere of influence, Jeter doubted that Eyer and himself would have been so humanely treated.

He had but to remember Kress to feel sure of this.

The altimeter said fifty thousand feet.

# CHAPTER VI
## STRATOSPHERE CURRENTS

Now the partner-scientists concentrated on the tremendous task of climbing higher than man had ever flown before. Nobody knew how high Kress had gone, for the only information which had come back had been the corpse of the sky pioneer. Jeter and Eyer hoped to land, too, but to be able to tell others, when they did, what had happened to them.

Somehow, away up here, the affairs of the Earth seemed trivial, unreal. What was the raising of an entire skyscraper—in reality so small that from this height it was difficult to pick out the biggest one through the telescope? What mattered a bridge across the Hudson that was really less than the footprint of an ant at this height?

Still, looking at each other, they were able to attain the old perspectives. Down there people like Jeter and Eyer were dying because of something that struck at them from somewhere up here in the blue darkness.

Their faces set grimly. The plane kept up its constant spiraling. Jeter and Eyer flew the ship in relays. Occasionally they secured the controls and allowed the plane to fly on, untended.

"But maybe we'd better not do too much of that," said Jeter dubiously. "I'm sure we are being observed, every foot of altitude we make. I don't care to run into something up here that will wreck us. Right now, Eyer, if we happened to be outside this sealed cabin instead of inside it, we'd die in less time than it takes to tell about it."

All known records for altitude—the only unknown one being Kress'—had now been broken by Jeter and Eyer. They informed Hadley of this fact.

"A week ago you'd have had headlines," came back Hadley. "To-day nobody cares, except that the world looks to you for information about this horror. The enemy is systematically destroying every building in Manhattan which dates back over eight years. Fortunately, save for the occasional die-hard who never believes anything, there are few deaths at the moment. But we're all waiting, holding our breaths, wondering what the next five minutes will bring forth. Is there any news there?"

How strange it seemed—as the altimeter said sixty-one thousand feet—to hear that voice out of the void. For under the plane there was no world at all, save through the telescope. Perhaps when morning came they would be able to see a little. Picard had reported the world to look flat from a little over fifty thousand-feet.

"No news, Hadley," said Jeter. "Except, that our plane behaves perfectly and we are at sixty-one thousand feet. Were it not for our turn and bank indicators, our altimeter and air speed instruments, and our navigational instruments, it would be impossible to tell—by looking at least, though we could tell by our shifting weight—whether we were upside down or right side up, on one wing or on an even keel. It's eery. We wouldn't be able to tell whether we were moving were it not for our air speed indicator. There are no clouds. The motor hum seems to be the only thing here—except ourselves of course—to remind us that we really belong down there with you."

T he connection was broken again as Jeter ceased speaking. Things seemed to be marking time on the ground, save for the strange demolitions of the unseen and apparently unknowable enemy. Would they ever really encounter him, or it?

When the sun came out of the east they leveled off at ninety thousand feet. By their reckoning they had scarcely moved in any direction from the spot where they had taken off. Jeter was satisfied that they were almost directly above Mineola. But the world had vanished. The plane rode easily on. Now and again it dipped one wing or the other—and even the veteran aviators felt a thrill of uneasiness. From somewhere up here in this immensity, Franz Kress had dropped to his death. Of course, if it had happened at this height he hadn't lived to suffer.

Or had he? What had been done to him by the—the denizens of the stratosphere?

Jeter sat down beside Eyer. It seemed strange to eat breakfast here, but the sandwiches and hot coffee in a thermos bottle were extremely welcome. They ate in silence, their thoughts busy. When they had made an end, Jeter squared his shoulders. Eyer grinned.

"Well, Lucian," he said, "are we in enemy territory by your calculations? And if so how do you arrive at your conclusions?"

"I'm still guessing, Tema," said Jeter, "but I've a feeling I'm not guessing badly, and.... Yes, we're somewhere within striking distance of the enemy, whatever the enemy is."

"What's the next move?

"We'll systematically cover the sky over an area which blankets New York, Long Island, Jersey City and surrounding territory for a distance of twenty miles. If we're above the enemy, perhaps we can look down upon him. We know he can't be seen from below, perhaps not even from above. If we are below him we'll try to fly into that column of his. What they'll do to us I.... You're not afraid to find out, are you?"

Eyer grinned. Jeter grinned back at him.

"What they'll do to us if we fly into them I'm sure I don't know. I don't think they'll kill our motor. If whoever or whatever controls the light column decides to us prisoners.... Well, we'll hope to have better luck combating them than Kress had."

And so begin that hours-long vigil of quartering the stratosphere over the unmarked area which Jeter had set as a limit. Now and again Hadley spoke to Jeter. Yes, the demolitions were still continuing in Manhattan. Could all telescopes on the ground pick out their space ship? Yes, said Hadley, and a young scientist in New Jersey was constantly watching them. Were they, since sunrise, ever out of his sight? Only when clouds at comparatively low altitudes intervened. However, the sky was unusually clear and it was hoped to keep their plane in sight during the entire day.

"Hadley," Jeter almost whispered, "I'm satisfied we're above the area of force, else we'd have flown into the anti-gravitation field. Get in touch with that Jersey chap by direct personal wire or radiophone if he is equipped with it. See that his watch is set with yours, which is synchronised with ours. Got that?"

"Yes."

"When you've done that give him these instructions: He is never to take his eyes of us for more than a split second at a time—unless someone else takes his place. I doubt if, at this distance, this will work, but it may help us a little. If we become invisible for even the briefest of moments, he is to look at his watch and observe the exact time, even to split seconds. We shall try to follow a certain plan hereafter in quartering the stratosphere, and I shall mark our location on the navigational charts every minute until we hear from this chap, or until we decide nothing is to be accomplished by this trick. Understand?"

"You're hoping that the enemy, while invisible to all eyes, yet has substance...."

"Shut up!" snapped Jeter, but he was glad that Hadley had grasped the idea. It was a slim chance, but such as it was it was worth trying. If the plane were invisible for a time, then it would be proof of some opaque obstruction between the plane and the eye of the beholder on the surface of the Earth. Refraction had to be figured, perhaps. Oh, there were many arguments against it.

The fliers followed the very outer edge of the area above the world they had mapped out as their limit of exploration. This circuit completed, they banked inward, shortening their circuit by about a mile of space. A mile, seen at a distance of ninety thousand feet, would be little indeed.

It was almost midday when they had their first stroke of luck.

The buzzer sounded at the very moment Eyer uttered an ejaculation.

"The Jersey fellow says there is nothing between his lens and your plane to obstruct the view."

"O.K.," retorted Jeter. "At the moment your buzzer sounded our plane suddenly jumped upward. That means an upcurrent of air indicating an obstruction under us. It must however, be invisible."

He severed the connection. His brow was furrowed thoughtfully. He was remembering Sitsumi and his rumored discovery.

They circled back warily. The eyes of both were fixed downward, staring into space. Their jaws were firmly set. Their eyes were narrowed.

And then....

There was that uprush of air again! It appeared to rise from an angle of about sixty degrees. They got the wind against their nose and started a humming dive, feeling in the alien updraft for the obstruction which caused it.

# CHAPTER VII

## INVISIBLE GLOBE

The buzzer of their radiophone was sounding, but so intent were they on this phenomenon they were facing, they paid it no heed. Their eyes were alight, their lips in firm straight lines of resolve, as they dived down upon the invisible obstruction—whatever it was—from whose surface the telltale updraft came.

It was Eyer who made the suggestion:

"Let's measure it to see what its plane extent is."

"How?" asked Jeter.

"Measure it by following the wind disturbance. We travel in one direction until we lose it. There is one extremity. In a few minutes we can discover exactly how big the thing is. What do you think it is?"

Jeter shook his head. There was no way of telling.

Jeter nodded agreement to Eyer. Then he spoke into the radiophone, telling Hadley what they had found, to which he could give no name.

"The world awaits in fear and trembling what you will have to report, Jeter," said Hadley. "What if you become unable to report, as Kress did?"

"Don't worry. We will or we won't. If we succeed we'll be back. If we fail, send up the other.... No, perhaps you hadn't better send up the new planes. But I think Eyer and I have a chance to discover the nature of this strange—whatever-it-is. If you can't contact us, delay twenty-four hours before doing anything. I—well, I scarcely know what to tell you to do. We'll just be shooting in the dark until we know what we're in for. You'll have to contain yourself in patience. What did you want with me?"

"Only to tell you of another strange news dispatch. It gives no details. It merely tells of strange activity around Lake Baikal, beyond the Gobi Desert. Queer noises at night, mysterious cordons of Eurasians to keep all investigators back, strange losses of livestock, foodstuffs...."

Jeter severed connection. There was little need to listen further to something which he couldn't explain yet, in any case.

Eyer, at the controls, banked the plane at right angles and flew on. In shortly less than a minute he banked again.

In five minutes he turned to Jeter with a queer expression on his face.

"Well," he said, "what's to do about it? What is it? It seems to be some solid substance approximately a quarter mile square. But it can't be true! A solid substance just hanging in the air at ninety thousand feet! It's beyond all imagining!"

"What man can imagine, man can do," replied Jeter. "A great newspaper editor said that, and we're going to discover now just how true it is."

"What's our next move?"

For a long time the partners, stared into each other's eyes. Each knew exactly what the other thought, exactly what he would propose as a course of action. Jeter heaved a sigh and nodded his head.

"We're as much in the power of the enemy here as we would be there, or anywhere else. We can't discover anything from here. Set the wheels down!"

"We can't tell anything about the condition of the surface of that stuff. We may crack up."

Jeter had to grin.

"Sounds strange, cracking up at ninety thousand feet, doesn't it? Well, hoist your helicopter vanes and drift down as straight as you can—but be sure and keep your motor idling."

Again they exchanged long looks.

"O.K.," said Eyer, as quietly as he would have answered the same order at Roosevelt Field. "Here we go!"

He pressed a button and the helicopters, set into the surface of the single sturdy wing, snapped up their shafts and began to spin, effectually slowing the forward motion of the plane. Eyer fish-tailed her with his rudder to help cut down speed.

"We can't see the surface of the thing at all, Lucian," said Eyer. "I'll simply have to feel for it."

"Well, you've done that before, too. We can manage all right."

Down they dropped. The updraft was now a cushion directly under them. And then their wheels struck something solid. The plane moved forward a few feet—with a strange sickening motion. It was as though the surface of this substance were globular. First one wheel rose, then dipped as the other rose. The plane came to rest on fairly even keel, and the partners, while the motor idled, stared at each other.

"Well?" said Eyer, a trace of a grin on his face.

"If it'll hold the plane it will hold us. Let's slide into our stratosphere suits and climb out. We have to get close to this thing to see what it is."

"Parachutes?" said Eyer.

Jeter nodded.

"It would simplify matters if the thing happened to tilt over and spill us off, I think," said Jeter, matching Eyer's grin with one of his own. "I can't think with any degree of equanimity of plunging ninety thousand feet without a parachute."

"I'm not sure I'd care for it with one," said Eyer.

They were soon in the tight-fitting suits which were customarily used by fliers who climbed above the air levels at which it was impossible for a human being to breathe without a supply of oxygen in a container. Their suits were sealed against cold. Set in their backs were oxygen tanks capable of holding enough oxygen for several hours. Over all this they fastened their parachutes.

Then, using a series of doors in order to conserve the warmth and oxygen inside their cabin, they let themselves out, closing each successive door behind them, until at last they faced the last door—and the grim unknown. They glanced at each other briefly, and Jeter's hand went forth to grasp the mechanism of the last door. Eyer stood at his side. Their eyes met. The door swung open.

They stepped down. The surface of this stratosphere substance was slippery smooth. Now that they stood on its surface they could sense something of its profile. Movement in any direction suggested walking on a huge ball. The queer thing was that they could feel but could not see. It was like walking on air. Their plane appeared to be suspended in midair.

For a moment Jeter had an overpowering desire to grab Eyer, jerk him back to the plane, and take off at top speed. But they couldn't do that, not when the world depended upon them. Had Kress encountered this thing? Perhaps. How must he have felt? He had been alone. These two were moral support for each other. But both were acutely remembering how Kress had come back.

And his plane? They'd perhaps discover what had happened to that too.

Eyer suddenly slipped and fell, as though he had been walking on a carpet which had been jerked from under his feet. From his almost prone position he looked up at Jeter. Jeter dropped to his knees beside him. Their covered hands played over the surface of their discovery, to find it smooth as glass. As though with one thought they placed their heads against it, right ears down, to listen. But the whole vast field seemed to be dead, lifeless. And yet—a solid it was, floating here in space—or just hanging. It seemed to be utterly motionless.

"There should be a way of discovering what this is, and why, and how it is controlled if an intelligence is behind it." Jeter spelled out the words in the sign language they had both learned as boys.

Eyer nodded.

They walked more warily when they had, traveling slowly and hesitantly, gone more than a hundred feet from their plane. They kept it in sight by constantly turning to look back. It was now several feet above them. No telling what might happen to them at any moment, and the plane was an avenue of escape.

They didn't wish to take a chance on stepping off into the stratosphere—and eternity.

"It's like an iceberg of space," said the fingers of Jeter. "But let's go back and look it over to the other side of the plane. We have to keep the plane in sight and work from it as a base. And say, what sort of sensations have you had about this surface we're standing on?"

Jeter could see Eyer's shudder as he asked the question. Slowly the fingers of his partner spelled out the answer.

"I've a feeling of eyes boring into my back. I sense that the substance under us is malignant, inimical. I have the same feeling with every step I take, as though the unseen surface were endowed with arms capable of reaching out and grabbing me."

"I feel it, too," said Jeter's fingers. "But I'm not afraid of fingers in the usual sense. I don't think of hands strangling us, or ripping us to shreds, but of quest-ing—well, call them tentacles, which may clasp us with gentleness even, and ab-sorb us, and annihilate us!"

Now the two faced each other squarely. Now they did not try to hide that their fear was an abysmal feeling, horrible and devastating.

"Let's get back to the plane and take off. We haven't a chance."

They clasped hands again and started running back, their plane their goal. Before they reached it they would change their minds, for they were not ordinarily lacking in courage—but so long as they ran both had the feeling of being pursued by malignant entities which were always just a step behind, but gaining.

They slipped on the smooth surface face and fell sprawling. Each felt, when he fell, that he must rise at once, with all his speed, lest something grasp him and hold him down forever. It was a horrible trapped feeling, and yet....

They had but to look at each other to see that they were free. Nothing gripped their feet to hold them back. Of course the way was slippery, but no more so than an icy surface which one essays in ordinary shoes. What then caused their fear?

T he plane, so plainly visible there ahead and above, was like a haven of refuge to them. They panted inside their helmets and their breath misted the glass of their masks. But they stumbled on, making the best speed they could under the circumstances.

Perhaps if they took, off, and regained their courage, returned to normal in surroundings they knew and understood, they could come back and try again, after having heard each other's voices. The silence, the sign manual, the odd, awe-some sensations, all combined to rob them of courage. They must get it back if they were to succeed. And they had been away from the plane for almost an hour. Hadley would be waiting for some news.

The plane was twenty yards away—and almost at the same time Eyer and Jeter saw something queer about it. At first it was hard to say just what it was.

They rushed on. They were within ten yards of the plane when a wail of anguish was born—and died—in two soundproof helmets. There was no questioning the fact that the plane had settled into the surface of the field.

The plane was invisible below the tops of the landing wheels, as though the plane were sinking into invisibility, slowly dissolving from the bottom.

"Understand?" Jeter's fingers almost shouted. "Understand why we felt the desire to keep moving? This field is alive, Eyer, and if we stand still it will swallow us just as it is swallowing our plane! Let's get in fast; maybe we can still pull free from the stuff and take off."

They were racing against time and in the heart of each was the feeling that whatever they did, their efforts would be hopeless. Still, the spinning propeller of their plane gave them strength to hope.

They went through the succession of doors as rapidly as they dared. Once in the comfort of their cabin they doffed their stratosphere suits with all possible speed. Jeter was the first free. He jumped to the controls and speeded up the motor. In a matter of seconds it was revving up to a speed which, had it been free, would have pulled the plane along at seven hundred miles an hour at the height at which they were.

But the plane did not move!

Jeter slowed the motor, then started racing it fast, trying to jerk the fuselage free of the imbedded wheels, but they would not be released. Both men realized that the wheels had sunk from sight while they had been delayed coming through the succession of doors—that the plane had sunk until the invisible surface gripped the floor of the fuselage.

Perspiration beaded the faces of both men. Eyer managed a ghastly grin. Jeter's brow was furrowed with frantic thought as he tried to imagine a way out.

"If we could somehow cut our landing gear free," began Jeter, "but—"

"But it's too late, Lucian," said Eyer quietly. "Look at the window."

They both looked.

Countless fingers of shadowy gray substance were undulating up the surface of the window, like pale angleworms or white serpents of many sizes, trying to climb up a pane of glass.

"Well," said Jeter, "here we are! You see? Outside we can see nothing. Inside we begin to see a little, and what good will it do us?"

Eyer grinned. It was as though he lighted a cigarette and nonchalantly blew smoke rings at the ceiling, save that they dared not use up any of their precious oxygen by smoking.

Their fear had left them utterly when it would have been natural for them to be stunned by it.

# CHAPTER VIII

## CATACLYSMIC HUNGER

Eyer thrust out his hand to cut the motor. Jeter stayed it.

"I've an idea," he said softly; "let it run. We'll learn something more about the sensitiveness of this material."

The motor was cut to idling. The plane scarcely trembled now in the pull of the motor, so firmly was she held in the grip of the shadowy, vague tentacles. A grim sort of silence had settled in the cabin. The faces of the two partners were dead white, but their eyes were fearless. They had come aloft to give their lives if need be. They wouldn't try to get them back now. Besides, what use was there?

Jeter paused for a moment in thought.

Then he began to examine some of their weapons. The only one by which they could fire outside the plane—due to the necessity of keeping the cabin closed to retain oxygen—was the rapid firer on the wing. This could be depressed enough to fire downward at an angle of forty-five degrees. Jeter hesitated for a moment.

He looked at Eyer. Eyer grinned. "It can't bring death to us any sooner," he said. "Let her go!"

Jeter tripped the rapid firer and held it for half a minute, during which time three hundred projectiles, eight inches long by two inches in diameter, were poured into the invisible surface. The bullets simply accomplished nothing. It was almost as though the field had simply opened its mouth to catch thrown food. There was no movement of the field, no jarring, no vibration. Nor did the plane itself tremble or shake. Jeter had to stop the rapid firer because its base, the plane, was now so firmly fixed that the recoil might kick the gun out of its mount.

Now the partners sat and looked out through the windows of unbreakable glass, watching the work of those tentacular fingers.

"How does it feel, Tema, to be eaten alive?" asked Jeter.

"Have you radiophoned Hadley about what's happening to us?"

"No," replied Jeter. "It would frighten the world half out of its wits. Besides, what can we say has caught us? We don't know."

"And what are we going to do about it?"

"We're going to wait. I've a theory about some of this. We know blamed well that, except for the most miraculous luck, you couldn't have set the plane down on this field without it slipping off again. Well there's only one answer to that: the rubbery resilience of the surface. It must have given a little to hold the plane—and us when we walked on it. What does that mean? Simply that we were seen and the field made usable for us by some intelligence. That intelligence watches us now. It saved our lives for some reason or other. It didn't destroy us when we were afoot out there. It isn't destroying us now. It's swallowing us whole—and for some reason. Why? That we'll have to discover. But I think we can rest easy on one thing. We're not to be killed by this swallowing act, else we'd have been dead before now."

"Have you any idea what this stuff is?"

"Yes, but the idea is so wild and improbable that I'm reluctant to tell you what I guess until I know more. However, if it develops that we are to die in this swallowing act, then I'll give you a tip—and it will probably knock you off your pedestal. But the more I think of it the more certain I am that the whole things is at least a variation of my idea. And the brains behind it, if my guess proves even approximately correct, will be too great for us to win mastery except by some miraculous accident favoring us—and true miracles come but seldom in these days."

"No? What do you call this?"

Jeter shrugged.

With many ports all around the cabin, all fitted with unbreakable glass, it was possible for the partners to see out in all directions. The tentacle fingers had now climbed up to a height sufficient to smother both windows. The fuselage was about half swallowed.

"I can almost hear the stuff sigh inwardly with satisfaction as it takes us in," said Eyer.

"I have the same feeling. There's a peculiar sound about it too; do you hear it?"

They listened. The sound which came into the cabin was such a sound as might have been heard by a man inside a cylinder lying on the bottom of a still pond. A whisper that was less than a whisper—a *moving* whisper. In it were life and death, and grim terror.

And then—remembering that contact with the propeller would shatter it, Tema cut the switch—the propeller stopped, the motor died, and utter silence, in the midst of an utter absence of vibration, possessed the comfortable little cabin. It was hard to believe. The cabin was a breath of home. It was a home. And it was being swallowed by some substance concerning which Eyer had no ideas at all and Jeter but a growing suspicion.

The plane sank lower and lower. The surface of the field was now almost to the top of the cabin doors. Most of the windows had been erased, but it made no particular difference in the matter of light. Jeter had put out his hand to snap on the lights, but stayed it when he saw that light came through to them.

Moment by moment the mystery of the swallowing deepened. It was like sinking into a snow bank. There was a sensation of smothering, though it was not uncomfortable because the cabin itself was self-sufficient in all respects to maintain life for a long period of time.

It was like sinking slowly into the depths of the sea.

The last port on the sides of the plane was erased. Now the two sat in their chairs and stared up at the ceiling, and at the glass-protected ports there. It was grim business. They almost held their breath as they waited.

At last those blurred tentacles began to creep across the lowest of the ceiling ports. Faster they came, and faster. In a few minutes every port was covered with a film of the weird stuff.

"It may be a foot deep above us," said Jeter. "I don't think we'll be able to tell how thick any bit of the stuff is. The surface of the field may be ten feet above our heads right now. Well, Tema, old son, we're prisoners as surely as though we were locked in a chrome steel vault a thousand feet underground. We can't go anywhere, or come back if we go there. We're prisoners, that's all—and all we can do is wait."

Eyer grinned.

Jeter began nonchalantly to slip off his helmet and goggles. He doffed his flying coat. In a short time the two might have been sitting over liquor and cigars in their own library at Mineola.

"Expecting company?" asked Eyer.

"Most emphatically," replied Jeter. "Company that is an unknown quantity. Company that will be wholly and entirely interesting."

So they waited. They could now feel themselves sinking faster into the substance. They settled on an even keel, however, but more rapidly than before, as though the directing intelligence behind all these had tired of showing them his wonders and was eager to get on with the business of the day.

Eyer happened to look down at one of the ports in the floor of the cabin.

"Good God!" he yelled, "Lucian!"

**H**e was pointing. His face had gone white again. His eyes were bulging. Jeter stared down into the floor ports—and gasped.

"I expected it, but it's a shock just the same, Tema," he said softly. "Get hold of yourself. You'll need all your faculties in a minute or two."

Through the ports they found themselves staring down all of twenty feet upon a milky white globe, set inside the greater, softer globe through which they were passing, like a kernel in a shell.

The plane was oozing through the "rind" which protected the strange globe below against the cold and discomfort of the stratosphere.

"They'd scarcely bring us this far to drop us, would they?" asked Eyer.

He was making a distinct effort to regain control of himself. His voice was normal, his breathing regular—and he had spoken thus to show Jeter that this was so.

"Whether we're to be dropped or lowered is all one to us," he said, "since we can do nothing in either case. Twenty feet of fall wouldn't smash us up much."

"Let's keep our eyes on the ceiling ports and see how this swallowing job is really done."

They alternately looked through the floor ports and the ceiling ports.

Under them the gray mass was crawling backward off the floor ports, leaving them clear. Now all of them were clear. Now the gray stuff began to vanish from the lower ports on either side of the cabin.

"I feel as though we were being digested and cast forth," said Jeter.

The action of the stuff was something like that. It had swallowed them in their entirety and now was disgorging them.

They watched the stuff move off the ports one by one, on either side. The lower ones were free. Then those next above, the gray substance retreating with what seemed to be pouting reluctance. Finally even the topmost ports were clear.

"The drop comes soon," said Eyer.

"Wait, maybe not."

T hey concentrated on the ceiling ports for a moment, but the clinging stuff did not vanish from them. They turned back to look through the floor ports. Right under them was the milky globe whose surface could easily accommodate their plane. If they had needed further proof of some guiding intelligence behind all this, that cleared space was it. They were being deliberately lowered to a landing place through a portion of the "rind" made soft in some mechanical way to allow the weight of their plane to sink through it.

They looked up again. Great masses of the gray substance still clung to the top of their cabin, like sticky tar. The substance was rubbery and lifelike in its resiliency, its tenacious grasp upon the Jeter-Eyer plane. By this means the plane was lowered to the "ground." Jeter and Eyer watched, fascinated, as the stuff slipped and lost its grip, and slowly retracted to become part of the dome above.

The plane had come through this white roof, bearing its two passengers, and now above them there was no slightest mark to show where they had come forth.

They rested on even keel atop the inner globe which they now could see was attached to the outer globe in countless places.

"I wonder if we dare risk getting out," said Eyer.

"I think so," said Jeter. "Look there!"

A trapdoor, shaped something like the profile of an ordinary milk bottle, was opening in the white globe just outside their plane. Framed in the door was a face. It was a dark face, but it was a human one—and the man's body below that face was dressed as simply, and in almost the same fashion, as were Jeter and Eyer themselves. He wore no oxygen tanks or clothing to keep out the cold.

The partners, lips firmly set, nodded to each other and began to open their doors. Imperturbably the dark man came to meet them.

Still other dark faces emerged from the door.

# CHAPTER IX
## A SCHEME IS DESCRIBED

The hands of the two wayfarers into the stratosphere dropped to their weapons as the men came through that door which masked the inner mystery of the white globe.

One of the men grinned. There was a threat in his grin—and a promise.

"I wouldn't use my weapons if I were in your place, gentlemen," he said. "Come this way, please. Sitsumi and The Three wish to see you at once."

Jeter and Eyer exchanged glances. Would it do any good to start a fight with these people? They seemed to be unarmed, but there were many of them. And probably there were many more beyond that door. Certainly this strange globe was capable of holding a small army at least.

Jeter shrugged. Eyer answered it with an eloquent gesture—and the two fell in with those who had come to meet them.

"How about our plane?" said Jeter.

"You need concern yourself with it no longer," replied one. "Its final disposal is in the hands of Sitsumi and The Three."

A cold chill ran along Jeter's spine. There was something too final about the guide's calm reply. Both adventurers remembered again, most poignantly, the fate of Kress.

The leaders stepped through the door. A flight of steps led downward.

Several of the swarthy-skinned folk walked behind Jeter and Eyer. There was no gainsaying the fact that they were prisoners.

Jeter and Eyer gasped a little as they looked into the interior of the white globe. It was of unusual extent, Jeter estimated, a complete globe; but this one was bisected by a floor at its center, of some substance that might, for its apparent lightness, have been aluminum. Plainly it was the dwelling place of these strange conquerors of the stratosphere. It might have been a vast room designed as the dwelling place of people accustomed to all sorts of personal comforts.

On the "floor" were several buildings, of the same material as the floor. It remained to be seen what these buildings were for, but Jeter could guess, he believed, with fair accuracy. The large building in the center would be the central control room housing whatever apparatus of any kind was needed in the working of this space ship. There were smaller buildings, most of them conical, looking oddly like beehives, which doubtless housed the denizens of the globe.

The atmosphere was much like that of New York in early autumn. It was of equable temperature. There was no discomfort in walking, no difficulty in breathing. Jeter surmised that at least one of those buildings, perhaps the central one, housed some sort of oxygen renewer. Such a device at this height was naturally essential.

The stairs ended. The prisoners and their guards stopped at floor level.

Jeter paused to look about him. His scientific eyes were studying the construction of the globe. The idea of escape from the predicament into which he and Eyer were plunged would never be out of his head for moment.

"Come along, you!"

Jeter started, stung by the savagery which suddenly edged the voice of the man who had first greeted him. There was contempt in it—and an assumption of personal superiority which galled the independent Jeter.

He grinned a little, looked at Eyer.

"I wonder if we have to take it," he said softly.

"It seems we might expect a little respect, at least," Eyer grinned in answer.

The guard suddenly caught Jeter by the shoulder.

"I said to come along!"

If the man had been intending to provoke a fight he couldn't have gone about it in any better way. Jeter suddenly, without a change of expression, sent a right fist crashing to the fellow's jaw.

"Don't use your gat, Eyer," he called to his partner. "We may kill a key man who may be necessary to our well-being later on. But black eyes and broken noses should be no bar to efficiency."

Without any fuss or hullabaloo, the dozen or so denizens of the globe who had met the partners closed on them. They came on with a rush. Jeter and Eyer stood back to back and slugged. They were young, with youthful joy in battle. They were trained to the minute. As fliers they took pride in their physical condition. They were out-numbered, but it was also a matter of pride with them to demand respect wherever they went. It was also a matter of pride to down as many of the attackers as possible before they themselves were downed.

It became plain that, though the denizens of the globe were armed with knives, they were not to be used. And it didn't seem they would be needed. The fighters were all muscular, well-trained fighters. But for the most part they fought in the manner of Chinese ta chaen, or Japanese ju-jutsu men. They used holds that were bone-breaking and it taxed the pair to the utmost to keep from being maimed by their killing strength.

The swarthy men were men of courage, no doubt about that. They fought with silent ferocity. They blinked when struck, but came back to take yet other blows with the tenacity of so many bulldogs. There was no gainsaying them, it seemed. They were here for the purpose of subduing their visitors and nothing short of death would stop them.

It wasn't courtesy, either, that failure to use knives, for Jeter saw murder looking out of more than one pair of eyes as their two pairs of fists landed on brown faces, smashed noses askew, and started eyes to closing.

"Their leader has them under absolute control—and that's a point for the enemy," Jeter panted to himself, as the strain of battle began to tell on him. "They've been instructed, no matter what we do, to bring us to their master or masters alive."

For a moment he toyed with the idea of drawing his weapon and firing point-blank into the enemy. He knew they would be compelled to take lives to escape—and that the lives of all these people were forfeit anyway because of the havoc which had descended upon New York City.

But he didn't make a move for his weapon. It would be sure death if he did, for the others were armed.

Brown men fell before the smashing of their fists. But the end of the fight was a foregone conclusion. Jeter had a bruised jaw. Eyer's nose was bleeding and one eye was closed when the reception committee finally came to close quarters, smothered them by sheer weight of numbers, and made them prisoners. Jeter's right wrist was manacled to Eyer's left with a pair of ordinary steel handcuffs. Their weapons were taken away from them now.

The leader of the committee, panting, but apparently unconcerned over what had happened, motioned the two men to lead the way. He pointed to the large building in the center of the "floor."

"That way," he said, "and I hope Sitsumi and The Three give us permission to throw you out without parachutes or high altitude suits."

"Pleasant cuss, aren't you?" said Eyer. "I don't think you like us."

The man would have struck Eyer for his grinning levity; but at that moment a door opened in the side of the large building and a man in Oriental robes stood there.

"Bring then here at once, Naka!" he said.

T he man called Naka, the leader whom Jeter had first struck, bowed low, with deep respect, to the man in the doorway.

"Yes, O Sitsumi!" he said. As he spoke he sucked in his breath with that snake-like hissing sound which is the acme of politeness, in Japan—"that my humble breath may not blow upon you"—and spread wide his hands. "They are extremely low persons and dared lay hands upon your emissaries."

Eyer grinned again.

"I think," he called, "there transpired what might be called a general laying on of hands by all hands."

"I deeply deplore your inclination to levity, Tema Eyer," said the man in the doorway. "It is not seemly in one whose intelligence entitles him to a place in our counsels."

Eyer looked at Jeter. What was the meaning of Sitsumi's cryptic utterance?

"Bring them in," snapped Sitsumi.

Jeter studied the man with interest. He knew instantly who he was and understood why Sitsumi had refused to answer his radio messages to Japan. He couldn't very well have done so in the circumstances. Here, under the broad dome of Sitsumi was probably the greatest scientific brain of the century. Jeter saw cruelty in his eyes too; ruthlessness, and determination.

The prisoners were marched into the room behind Sitsumi, who stepped aside, looking curiously at Jeter and Eyer as they passed him. Inside the door, pausing only a moment to glance over the big room's appointments, Jeter turned on Sitsumi.

"Just what do you intend doing with us, Sitsumi?" he asked. "I suppose it's useless to ask you, also, what the meaning of all this is?"

"I shall answer both your questions, Jeter," said Sitsumi. "Step this way, please. The Three should hear our conference."

They were conducted into a smaller room. Its floors were covered with skins. There were easy chairs and divans. It might have been their own luxuriously appointed rooms at Mineola. At a long table three men—all Orientals—were deeply immersed in some activity which bent their heads absorbedly over the very center of the table. It might have been a three-sided chess game, by their attitudes.

"Gentlemen!" said Sitsumi.

The three men turned.

"My colleagues, Wang Li, Liao Wu and Yung Chan," Sitsumi introduced them. "Without them our great work would have been impossible."

**H**ere were the three missing Chinese scientists. Jeter and Eyer had seen many pictures of them. Jeter wondered whether their adherence to Sitsumi were voluntary or forced. But it was voluntary, of course. The three brains of these brilliant men could easily have outwitted Sitsumi had they been unwilling to associate themselves with him. The three Orientals bowed.

Jeter and Eyer were bidden to take chairs side by side. The guards drew back a little but never took their eyes off the two. Sitsumi ranged himself beside his colleagues at the table.

"I'll answer your questions now, gentlemen, in the presence of my colleagues so that you shall know that we are together in what we propose. We wish you to join us. The only alternative is ... well, you recall what happened to your countryman, Kress? The same, or a similar fate, will be yours if you don't ally yourselves with us."

Jeter and Eyer exchanged glances.

"Just what *are* you doing?" asked Jeter. "I've seen some of the results of your activities, but I can see no reason for them. I would pronounce everything you have done so far to be the acts of madmen."

"We are not mad," said Sitsumi. "We are simply a group of people of mixed blood who deplore the barriers of racial prejudice, for one thing. We are advocates of a deliberately contrived super-race, produced by the amalgamation of the best minds and the best bodies of all races. We ourselves are what the world calls Eurasians. In our youth people patronised us. In Asia we were shunned. We were shunned everywhere by both races from which we trace our ancestry. We are not trying to be avenged upon the world because we have been pariahs. We are not so petty. But by striving until we have become the world's four greatest scientists we have proved to our own satisfaction that a mixture of blood is a wholesome thing. This expedition of ours, and its effect so far on New York City, is the result of our years of planning."

"I see no need for wholesale murder. Lecture platforms are open to all creeds, all races...."

Something suggestive of a sneer creased Sitsumi's lips. The Three did not change expression in the least.

"**P**eople do not listen to reason. They listen to force. We will use force to make them listen, in the end, to reason—backed in turn by force, if you like. We have settled on New York from which to begin our conquest of the world because it is the world's largest, richest, most representative city. If we control New York we control the wealth of the North American continent, and therefore the continent itself. Our destruction of buildings in New York City serves a twofold purpose. It prepares the inhabitants to listen to us later because, seeing what we are capable of doing, they will be afraid not to. Our efficiency is further shown in our destruction of the old out-of-date buildings, chosen for destruction simply because they are obsolete. The New York City of our schemes will be a magic city...."

"But what is your purpose, in a few words?" insisted Jeter.

"The foundation of a world government; the destruction of the mentally deficient; the scientific production of a mixed race of intellectuals, comparable to, but greater than, that of ancient Greece, which was great because it was a human melting pot."

"How are you going to do it—after you've finished your grandstand plays?" said Eyer.

Sitsumi stared at Eyer, his eyes narrowing. Eyer was making his dislike entirely too plain. Jeter nudged him, but the question had been asked.

"With this space ship—and others which are building," replied Sitsumi. "Haven't you guessed at any of our methods?"

"Yes," said Jeter, "I know you are the rumored inventor of a substance which is invisible because light rays are bent around it instead of passing through, yet the result is as though they actually passed through. I judge that the shell, or skin, of this stratosphere ship is composed of this substance, whose formula of construction is your secret. Light rays passing around it would render it invisible, yet would make the beholding eye seem to see in a straight line as usual, disregarding refraction."

Sitsumi nodded. The Three nodded with him, like puppets. But their eyes were glowingly alive.

"You are right. Are you further interested? If you have no interest in our theories there is little need to pursue our plans further, where you are concerned."

"We are interested, of course," said Jeter. "We are interested in your theories, without committing ourselves to acceptance of them; and we are naturally interested in saving our lives. Let us say then, for the moment, that we do not refuse to join you."

# CHAPTER X

## HOW IT CAME ABOUT

"You will have twenty-four hours in which to decide whether to join us," was Sitsumi's ultimatum. "We would not allow you five minutes were it not that our cause would be benefited by the addition of your scientific knowledge."

Sitsumi did not repeat the alternative. Remembering Kress, Jeter and Eyer did not need to ask him. There was but one alternative—death—a particularly horrible one. That Sitsumi and the Three would not hesitate was amply proved. Already they were guilty of the death of thousands. They were in deadly earnest with their scheme for a world government.

Jeter and Eyer were kept shackled together, and were, in addition, chained to the floor of the main room of the white globe with leg irons. Their keys were in the hands of Naka, whose hatred of Jeter for hitting him on the jaw was so malevolent it fairly glowed from his eyes like sparks shot forth.

Food was brought them when asked for. It wasn't easy to partake of it, because their manacled hands had to be moved together, which made it extremely awkward.

Jeter and Eyer set themselves the task of trying to figure some way out in the twenty-four hours of life still left them if they failed. That Hadley, down in New York City, and all the best minds who were cooperating with Jeter and Eyer in their mad effort to avert world catastrophe, would make every effort to come to their assistance by sending up the planes which must even now be nearing completion, they hadn't the slightest doubt.

Would they arrive in time? Even if they did, was there anything they could possibly do to save themselves? Surely this space ship must be vulnerable. Else why did it climb so high into the stratosphere? It was far beyond the reach of ordinary planes. High trajectory projectiles had slight chance of hitting it, even if it were visible. What then was its vulnerability, which this hiding seemed to indicate? They must know within twenty-four hours.

So they sat side by side, watching events unfold. The Three talked mandarin. Eyer, for all his levity, was a man of unusual attainments. He understood mandarin, for one thing—a fact which even Jeter did not know at first. The Chinese never seemed even to consider that either of them might know the tongue. Chinese seldom found foreigners who did comprehend them. In only so much were The Three in the least bit careless.

Eyer strained his ears to hear everything which passed between Sitsumi and the Three. Both men listened to any chance words in English or French on the part of all hands within the globe which might give them a hint.

And in those twenty-four hours the sky-scientists learned much.

They conversed together, when they spoke of important matters which they wished hidden from their captors, out of the corners of their mouths after the method of criminals. They used it with elaborate unconcern. They might have seemed to be simply staring into space at such moments, dreading approaching death perhaps, and simply twiddling their fingers. But by each other every word was clearly heard.

"That last outburst of Sitsumi's explains a lot of the reported activity in the Lake Baikal region, beyond the Gobi," swiftly dropped from Jeter's lips. "The materials which Sitsumi uses in the preparation of his light-ray-bending substance are found near there somehow. And that means that the Japanese guards — which may be Eurasian guards, after what Sitsumi told us — and employees of this unholy crowd, are easily engaged in the preparation of other space ships."

"Does this thing seem to have any armament?" asked Eyer.

Jeter signified negation with a swift movement of his head.

"Their one weapon seems to be the apparatus which causes that ray. You know, the ray which lifts buildings, pulling them up by the roots."

"Have you any idea what it is?"

"Yes. That last stuff of the Three which you translated for me gives me a clue. At first I thought that they had perfected some substance, perhaps with unknown electrical properties, which nullified gravity. But that won't prove out. If the ray simply nullified gravity, the buildings down there, while weightless, would not rise as they did. They might sway if somebody breathed against them. A midget might lift one with his finger; but they wouldn't fly skyward as they did — and do!"

For a moment the partners ceased their whispering and talked together naturally to disarm suspicion. The fact that the space ship and its ruthless denizens still engaged in the awful work of devastation was amply being proved. In the main room it was possible, through the use of telescopes and audiphones — set into the walls so that they were invisible, yet enabled any one in the room to see everything, and hear everything that transpired on the far earth below — to keep close watch on the work of the destroyers. Anything close enough could be seen with the naked eye through the walls of the globe.

Now the space ship was systematically destroying buildings the length and breadth of Manhattan Island. The river-front buildings were destroyed in a single sweep, from north to south, of the ghastly ray. Farther back from the Hudson, however, after the water-front buildings had been reduced to mere piles of rubble, the most beautiful, most modern buildings were left standing.

"Can't you just imagine those beautiful structures filled with the monsters created by the genius of Sitsumi and the Three—and their as yet unknown lieutenants back at Lake Baikal?"

Eyer gritted his teeth. His hands closed atop the table at which they were seated. The knuckles went white with the strain. The lips of both men were white. They realized to the full the dreadful responsibility which they had assumed. They knew how abysmally hopeless was their chance of accomplishing anything. And without some gigantic effort being made, the world as they knew it would be destroyed. In its place would be a race of strange beings, of vengeful hybrids endowed from birth with the will to conquer, or destroy utterly.

"You were speaking of the levitating ray," prompted Eyer with swift change to the sidewise whispering.

"From what you heard I'm sure it is something invented by Liao Wu, Yung Chan and Wang Li. In so much they have an advantage over Sitsumi. I doubt if there is any love lost among them, beyond the fact that they need one another. Sitsumi is master of the substance which bends light rays—and thus is rendered invisible, while the Three are masters of the ray which not only propels this space ship, but is the agency by which buildings are torn up, dropped and destroyed. It's plain to me that this room is the control room of the space ship. The ray is—well, it's as difficult to explain as electricity, and perhaps as simple in its operation. The ray does more than nullify gravity—can be made to reverse gravity! Let's call the ray the gravity inverter for want of a better name. It makes anything it touches literally *fall away from the Earth*, toward the point whence the ray emanates!"

"And if we were to obtain control of the apparatus which harnesses the ray?"

"We lack the knowledge of the Three for its operation. No, we've got to find some simpler solution in the brief time we have."

At this point the partners had been within the white globe about ten hours and they had learned much about it. The inner globe, for example, maintained an even keel, no matter how the space ship as a whole moved on its rays that seemed like table legs. The gyroscopic principle was used. The inner globe was movable within the outer globe, or rind. If for any reason the space ship listed in one direction or the other, the inner globe, while it rose and fell naturally, remained upright, its floor always level so that, the gyroscope controlling the whole, the central, levitating, ray would always, must always, as it proved, point downward.

Try as they might, the partners could not see how the Three manipulated the ray. They guessed that there were many buttons on the table at which they sat. The table itself was not an ordinary table. What might have been called a fifth leg, squarely under the center of the table, was about three feet square. Through this, Jeter guessed, ran the wires by which they controlled all their activities, machinery to operate which had been installed under the floor in the unseen lower half of the inner globe.

They knew that must remain forever a secret from them.

There was a sudden stir among the Three. Jeter and Eyer turned aside for a moment to peer down upon New York City. They held their breath with horror as they saw the smoking devastation which must have buried thousands of people. The wrecking had been all but complete. Only the finest buildings still stood. Jeter wondered why the falling back of the shattered buildings had not shaken down those which the Sitsumi crowd had not wished to destroy. The repeated shocks must almost have shaken Manhattan Island on its foundations.

They saw what had caused the sudden stiffening of the Three. Sitsumi, busily engaged at something else nearby, quietly approached the Three.

"What is it?" he asked.

"Rescue planes," said Wang Li. "New York City sends six fliers to rescue Jeter and Eyer. New planes. They'll reach us, Sitsumi. We should have thought to destroy all dangerous air ports. A fatal oversight!"

Sitsumi's eyes were grave. He looked at each of the Three in turn.

"God!" said Jeter's whispering lips. "If we could read their minds! If only we could guess what it is they fear, we'd have the secret by which we might destroy them."

"They're vulnerable," said Eyer, "but how?"

"Watch!" said Jeter. "Listen! And here's to those six unknowns coming up to, maybe, get the same dose we're due for! We were closely watched. New York City knows exactly where we vanished in the sky. Those six planes are aiming at us—at a spot in the stratosphere they can't see. And yet, why should Sitsumi and the Three be so fearful? All they have to do is move a half mile in any direction and they'll never find them."

"But to move will interfere with their plans," said Eyer. "Lucian, look at the expressions on their faces! Something tells me they are vulnerable in ways we haven't guessed at. If we knew the secret maybe we could destroy them. We've got to discover their weak spot."

There was a long pause while Jeter and Eyer watched the rescue ships come climbing up the endless stairways of the sky. Then Jeter whispered again, guardedly as usual.

"There seems to be nothing we can do. If our friends are able, by some miracle, to do something, you know what that means to us?"

"It means we're as good as dead no matter what happens," replied Eyer. "But we're only two—and there must be a million buried under the debris in New York City alone. If we can do anything at all...."

There he left it. The partners looked at each other. Each read the right answer in the other's eyes. When the showdown came they'd die as cheerfully as they knew how, hoping to the last to do something for the people who must still hope that, somehow, they would cause this bitter cup of catastrophe to pass from them. And there were thousands upon thousands whose blood cried out for vengeance.

The hours sped as the six planes fled upward. To the ears of the partners, through the audiphones, came the stern roaring of their motors. In their eyes they bulked larger and larger as the time fled away.

The sand in the hour glass was running out. When it was all gone, and the time had come, what could the helpless Jeter and Eyer hope to accomplish?

For an hour they studied the concerned faces of Sitsumi and the Three.

They were fearful of something.

What?

# CHAPTER XI

## TO THE RESCUE

"Why should we run?" the voice of Sitsumi suddenly rang out in the control room. "Must we admit in the very beginning of our revolution that we are vulnerable? Must we confess the fears to which all humanity is heir? We had not thought ourselves liable to attack, but there still is a way to destroy these upstarts. To your places, everyone! We shall fight these winged upstarts and destroy them!"

The denizens of the space ship were at their stations. Jeter and Eyer could imagine the minions of Sitsumi and the Three, below the floor of the white globe, standing-to on platforms about the unseen engines which gave life and movability to this ship of the stratosphere. How many there were of them there was no way of knowing. They had guessed two hundred. There might have been a thousand. It scarcely mattered.

Sitsumi's face was set in a firm mask. He, of all the "lords of the stratosphere," seemed to possess endless courage. His example fired the three.

"What do you plan?" asked Wang Li.

Jeter and Eyer listened with all their ears.

"We have only one weapon in this unexpected emergency," said Sitsumi quietly. "We cannot direct the ray upward or laterally: it is not so constructed. But we can attack with the space ship itself! And remember that so long as our outer rind remains intact and hard we are invisible to attackers."

Jeter and Eyer exchanged glances.

"If only we could find the way to break or soften that outer rind," said Jeter.

"What can we do?" asked Eyer. "If it is impervious to the cold of these heights; if it is so strong that it is impervious to the tremendous pressure inside the globe—which must be kept at a certain degree to maintain human life—what can we do? We tried bullets. We might as well have used peas and pea-shooters. If our friends try bombs they will still be unsuccessful. If only we could somehow open up the outer rind or soften it, so that our friends could see the inner globe and reach it with their bombs!"

Jeter's face was now dead white. His eyes were aglow with excitement.

"Tema," he whispered, "Tema, that's their vulnerability! That's what they fear! They're scared that the outer rind may be broken—which would spell destruction to the space ship and everybody in it."

"Including us," replied Eyer, "but, anyway—well, what's the odds? We're only two—and with this thing destroyed the nightmare will end. Of course there should be some way to raid the Lake Baikal area and destroy any other ships in the making, besides ferreting out the secret of the invisible substance and the elements of the gravity inverter. If we somehow survive, and this ship is destroyed, that's the next thing to do."

Jeter nodded and signaled Eyer to cease whispering.

They devoted their attention now to the six planes. They were coming up in battle formation. They were in plain view and through the telescopes it could be seen that each was armed with bombs of some kind. Useless against the invisible space ship as matters now stood; but what would those bombs do to the inner globe?

It still lacked several hours of the time allowed in the ultimatum to Jeter and Eyer of Sitsumi and the Three, when the six planes leveled off within a couple of miles of the space ship. They knew about where the stratosphere had swallowed up Jeter and Eyer. Now they were casting about for a sign, like bloodhounds seeking the spoor of an enemy.

Jeter and Eyer held their breaths as they watched. Now and again they stole glances at Sitsumi and the Three, who were watching the six planes with the intensity of eagles preparing to dive.

Naka stepped up close to Jeter.

"When the time comes," he said menacingly, "and it appears that we may be in difficulties with the fools who think to thwart Sitsumi and the Three and rescue you, it shall give me great pleasure to destroy you with your own automatic."

"Pleasant fellow," said Eyer. "Shall I smash him, Lucian?"

Jeter shook his head.

"Our friends out there will look after that, Tema," he said in a natural tone of voice. "I'll bet you two to one they get this ship within an hour. Not that a bet will mean anything, as they'll get us, too!"

"Your friends," said Naka, "will be destroyed. They will not even be given the opportunity you were given. Sitsumi and the Three will waste but little time on them!"

"What," said Jeter calmly "is Sitsumi's hurry? Why is he scared?"

"Scared?" Naka seemed on the point of hitting Jeter for the blasphemy. "Scared? He fears nothing. We'll down your friends long before their motors—"

Sitsumi suddenly turned and looked at Naka. The look in Sitsumi's eyes was murderous, Naka went dead white.

"I think your master believes you talk too much, Naka," said Jeter, but Jeter's eyes were gleaming, too.

As soon as Sitsumi had turned back to his station Jeter's lips began to move.

"See?" he said. "It isn't their machine guns these people fear. It isn't their bombs—it's their motors! I wonder why...."

**B**y now the six planes were flying abreast, in battle formation, almost above the space ship, at perhaps a thousand feet greater elevation. A strange humming sound was traveling through the space ship. The whole inner globe was vibrating, shaking—and vibration was a menace to glass or crystal!

"We've got the answer!" said Jeter. "The outer rind, while capable of being softened—in sections at least, with safety—for special reasons, such as happened when we were 'swallowed,' can be hardened to the point of disruption. It can be shattered, Tema, by vibration! That's why the space ship keeps far above the roar of cities! The humming of countless automobile engines might shatter the rind! God, I hope this is the answer!"

In his mind's eye Eyer could picture it—the outer rind "freezing" solid, and cracking with the thunderous report of snapping ice on a forest lake. No wonder Sitsumi and the Three must destroy the six planes.

"Now!" yelled Sitsumi. "Shift positions! The space ship will be hurled directly at the formation of planes! Wang Li, to the beam controls!"

Wang Li sprang to the table, pressed a button. The humming sound in the space ship grew to mighty proportions. The trembling increased.

Jeter and Eyer kept their eyes glued to the six planes above. Without tilting their noses the six planes seemed to plunge straight down toward the surface of the space ship. Thus the two knew that the space ship was in motion—itself being bodily hurled, as its only present weapon of offense, against the earthling attackers.

A split second—

One of the planes struck the surface solidly and crashed. Instantly its wheels and its motor were caught in the outer rind.

The other five ships scattered wildly, escaping the collision by some sixth sense, or through pure chance.

"Poor devil!" said Jeter. "But his buddies can see his plane and know that it marks the spot where they could conveniently drop their bombs."

Eyer was on the point of nodding when Sitsumi shouted.

"Quickly, Wang Li! Spin the outer shell before the enemy uses the wrecked plane as an aiming point!"

**A** whirring sound. The plane whirled around as though it were twirled on the end of a string. To the five other pilots it must have seemed that the plane had struck some invisible obstruction, been smashed, and now was whirling away to destruction after a strange, incomprehensible hesitation in the heart of the stratosphere.

"Quickly, you fool!" shouted Sitsumi at Wang Li. "You're napping! You should have got all those planes! And you should have spun the outer globe instantly, before the remaining enemy had a chance to find out our location."

"I can move away a half mile," suggested Wang Li.

"We've got to silence those motors, fool!" yelled Sitsumi. "You know very well that we can't run. Charge them again, and take care this time that you crash into the middle of their formation."

"They're scattered over too great an area. I should wait for them to reform."

"Fool! Fool! Don't you think I know the weakness in my own invention? The proper vibration will destroy us! If the rind is softened we become visible. We dare not wait for them to reform! Attack each plane separately if necessary, and at top speed!"

Jeter began to speak rapidly out of the corner of his mouth. Even Naka's attention was fastened on the five planes and Wang Li's efforts to destroy them.

"Gag Naka!" said Jeter. "The keys! In some way we've got to get to our plane. It's barely possible. If we can start the motor.... Hurry! Now, while the whole outfit is watching our friends out there!"

Eyer rose and reached for Naka with his right hand.

He dared not miss his lunge. He did not. His huge hand fastened in the throat of their keeper. Nobody—neither Sitsumi nor the Three—turned as Naka gasped and struggled. Eyer pulled the man back over the table and, his neck thus within reach of both hands, snapped it as he would have broken the neck of a chicken.

Jeter was already searching the body for the keys. He found them.

Their leg irons were just falling free when Sitsumi turned. Eyer was feeling for the automatics in Naka's belt.

"We won't need them!" yelled Jeter. "There isn't time. Let's go!"

Jeter was away at top speed, almost pulling Eyer off his feet because their hands were still fastened together with the handcuffs.

They were outside on the floor level.

And through many doors denizens of the lower control room, hurried out by the commands of Sitsumi, were racing to head them off. But nothing could stop them. One man got in their way and Eyer's right fist caved in his face with one deadly, devastating blow. They had now reached the stairs.

T he space ship was being hurled at the five remaining planes. Even as the two men reached the stairs and started up, another of the dauntless rescuers paid with his life for his courage. Several bombs exploded as his plane struck the space ship, but they caused no damage whatever. The hard outer rind seemed to be impervious to the explosions. Obviously no explosive could destroy the space ship.

"Quickly, Tema," said Jeter. "The rind can be shattered by vibration, and we've got to do it somehow."

"And after that?" panted Eyer.

"Our friends out there can then see the inner globe. They'll drop bombs. They'll smash in the globe and—"

"I know," said Eyer. "Its inhabitants, including us, will start off in all directions through the stratosphere, with great speed, and probably in many pieces."

Jeter laughed. Eyer laughed with him. They didn't fear death, for now they felt they were on the verge of destroying this monster of space.

Their pursuers were following them closely.

Jeter frantically tried to unfasten the handcuffs as they ran. He didn't manage it until the door was almost reached. He left one cuff dangling on his right wrist.

Then, they were through the door.

"Now, Tema," shouted Jeter, "if you believe in God—if you have faith—pray for strength to move this plane!"

"Where?"

"So that its wheels and nose go through this open door! Then it won't travel forward when we start the motor—and our pursuers won't be able to get through to stop us."

"You think of everything, don't you?" There was a grin on Eyer's face. But his eyes were stern. He wasn't belittling their deadly danger. And there was also a chance that Jeter's vibration idea was wrong.

"Those four planes," panted Jeter, as the two tried to get their plane in motion toward the door, "cause, from a distance, through thin air, a slight vibration, varying with their distance from the globe; our plane motor racing and actually in contact with the globe, can set up a tremendous vibration by its great motor speed. If we can vibrate the globe up to its shattering point there's a chance!"

"We can't pull her, Lucian," said Eyer. "I'll do a Horatius at the door. You get in, start the motor, taxi her until the wheels go through. I'll keep the crowd back."

"Right!"

Jeter went through the doors into the plane. In a few seconds the propeller kicked over, hesitated, kicked again. Then the motor coughed, coughed again, and broke into a steady roaring.

# CHAPTER XII

## HIGH CHAOS

The plane moved forward. Its tail swung around. Its wheels headed for the door. They dropped through, into the faces of the foremost pursuers, all of whom were thus effectually blocked off.

The plane was held as in a vise. The propeller vanished in a blur as Jeter let the motor out. It was humming an even, steady note. The doors came open again.

Jeter came out, his eyes glowing.

"We haven't the chance of the proverbial celluloid dog chasing the asbestos cat," he shouted to be heard above the roar of the motor. "But grab your high altitude suit, oxygen container, and parachute, and let's get as far away from this plane as we can. Who knows? When the end comes we may get a break at that!"

They ran until the bulge of the inner globe all but hid the plane from them. They could see only the top wing. They did not go farther because they wished to make sure that the enemy did not dislodge the plane and nullify all their work.

"They won't be able to," said Jeter, "for that motor is pulling against the wheels and holding them so tight against the side of that door that a hundred men couldn't budge the plane. But we can't take chances."

Quickly the partners slipped into their suits, adjusted their oxygen tanks and parachutes. Then Jeter slipped back the elastic sleeve of his suit and motioned Eyer to do the same. The manacles were brought into view again. They looked at each other. Eyer grinned and held out his left hand. Jeter snapped the second cuff to Eyer's wrist.

The act was significant.

Whatever happened to them, would happen to both in equal measure. It was a gesture which needed no words. If they were slain when their friends—if their theory was correct—finally saw the space ship, they would die together. If by some miracle they were hurled into outer space and lived to use their parachutes—well, the discomfort was a small price to pay to stay together.

Now they devoted all their attention to their own situation. Four planes still spun warily above the space ship. Wang Li was patently trying with all his might to get all four of them before the Jeter-Eyer plane, by shattering the rind, disclosed the inner core to the bombs of the remaining planes.

"Lucian!" said the fingers of Eyer. "Can you tell whether anything is happening to the rind?"

Jeter hesitated for a long time. There was a distinct and almost nauseating vibration throughout all the space ship. And was there not something happening to the rind over a wide area, directly above the Jeter-Eyer plane?

They could fancy the snapping of ice on a forest lake in mid-winter.

They couldn't hear, in their suits. They could only feel. But all at once the outer rind, above their plane, vanished. At the same instant the plane itself, propeller still spinning, rose swiftly up through the hole in the rind. The air inside the globe was going out in a great rush.

The partners looked at each other. At that moment the four planes swooped over the space ship....

Jeter and Eyer knew that the inner globe had at last become visible, for from the bellies of the four planes dropped bomb after bomb. They fell into the great aperture. Jeter and Eyer flung themselves flat. But the bombs had worked sufficient havoc. They had removed all protection from the low-pressure stratosphere. The air inside the space ship went out with a rush. Jeter and Eyer, hearing nothing, though they knew that the explosions must have been cataclysmic, were picked up and whirled toward that opening, like chips spun toward the heart of a whirlpool.

But for their space suits they would have been destroyed in the outrush of air. Out of the inner globe came men that flew, sprawled out, somersaulting up and out of apertures made by the crashing bombs. Ludicrous they looked. Blood streamed from their mouths. Their faces were set in masks of agony. There were Sitsumi and, one after another, the Three.

Then fastened together by the cuffs, the partners were being whirled over and over, out into space. Their last signals to each other had been:

"Even if you're already dead, pull the ripcord ring of your chute!"

Crushed, buffeted, they still retained consciousness. They sought through the spinning stratosphere for their rescuers. Thousands of feet below — or was it above? — they saw them. Yes, below, for they looked at the tops of the planes. Their upward flight had been dizzying. They waited until their upward flight ceased.

Then, as they started the long fall to Earth, they pulled their rings and waited for their chutes to flower above them.

Soon they were floating downward. Side by side they rode. Above them their parachutes were like two umbrellas, pressed almost too closely together.

They looked about them, seeking the space ship.

The devastation of its outer rind had been complete, for they now could see the inner globe, and it too was like — well, like merely part of an eggshell.

The doomed space ship — gyroscope still keeping the ray pointed Earthward — describing an erratic course, was shooting farther upward into the stratosphere, propelled by the ghastly ray which, now no longer controlled by Wang Li, drove the space ship madly through the outer cold.

Far below the partners many things were falling: broken furnishings of mad dreamers' stratosphere laboratories, parts of strange machines, whirling, somersaulting things that had once been men.

The partners looked at each other.

The same thought was in the mind of each, as the four remaining planes came in toward them to convoy them down—that when the lords of the stratosphere finally reached the far Earth, only God would know which was Sitsumi and who were the Three.

Lector House believes that a society develops through a two-fold approach of continuous learning and adaptation, which is derived from the study of classic literary works spread across the historic timeline of literature records. Therefore, we aim at reviving, repairing and redeveloping all those inaccessible or damaged but historically as well as culturally important literature across subjects so that the future generations may have an opportunity to study and learn from past works to embark upon a journey of creating a better future.

This book is a result of an effort made by Lector House towards making a contribution to the preservation and repair of original ancient works which might hold historical significance to the approach of continuous learning across subjects.

HAPPY READING & LEARNING!

**LECTOR HOUSE LLP**
E-MAIL: lectorpublishing@gmail.com

9 789353 366179